# THE LOVE BOYZ

First of a Trilogy

BY

Derrion Dante' Robinson

This is a work of fiction. All events in this story are solely the product of the author's imagination. Any similarities between any characters and situations in this book to any individuals, living or deceased, or actual places and situations are purely coincidental.

Edited by: "12Thirteen14"

Cover Art by: "Nicely Done Productions"

# *ACKNOWLEDGMENTS*

First and foremost, I give all thanks and glory to my creator, "JAH" (GOD). Because it is him who dwells and works through me that I am able to accomplish the goal, I set out for my sons. Although they were here only for a brief moment, I intend to allow my sons the opportunity to not only mark their footprints in the world but also in the minds and hearts of others.

I also would like to thank their mother, Brandie (My Queen) for carrying and blessing me with my two young Princes.

To those who helped bring this book to life, their grandmother, Misty (My mother), I am grateful for all the hard work and effort she has given to help me accomplish this task. Thanks, Ms. Victoria Christopher Murray for the professional guidance and feedback on this project and thanks to my cousin, Tevyn, for bringing my vision to life with his graphic skills.

I would like to give a very special thanks to my grandmothers; Zola & Suzanne for the constant prayers.

To my Biological Father, Brian D. Robinson, even though we have not always seen eye to eye, probably due to the fact that we are so much alike, I want to acknowledge you. For without you, there would be no me.

To the remainder of my family, Aunts, (Pat and Yolanda), Uncle, (Nathan), Brother, (Cameron), Sisters, (Brianna and Shanika), Step Pops, (Keith) and my Cousins (Alondria, Koreana and Marco), I am extremely grateful for the fact that you have never given up on me and have always given me unconditional love. You all are the ones that make up and complete my family, and my loyalty is forever with you all. I love you all regardless if we're battling a storm or sitting on a beach enjoying the sunshine. Anybody that I missed, please charge it to my mind and not my heart.

Last but certainly not least, to my family and friends that are accompanying my sons in the afterlife, I want to say "I miss ya'll and until I see ya'll again, please do me a favor and watch over my sons as you all continue to watch over me." One.

Peace, Love & Blessings

*Derry Don*

13.D.K.D.14

**"A Note To The Reader"**

As it was pointed out to me, most or all fictional books do not contain Real names. However, in some instances, this one does. As a father who lost two sons before they were able to take their first steps, I set out on a mission to give Kevion and Devion voices that would be heard by the one's that read this book. I would like to thank you for spending your time with my boys, and I do hope and pray that you enjoy every minute of it.

To: Mrs. [illegible]

From: #14 [illegible]

FB @ The Love Boyz Book

FB@ The Love Boys Book

# Chapter 1

Clutching his chrome-plated forty-five, Kevion Love was keeping one eye on the road and the other watching a white two-door Bentley coupe that had been cautiously trailing him and his twin brother, Devion. They'd been followed for the last twenty or so minutes, ever since leaving their mother's house in North Dallas.

"Hey bro, go ahead and go to the hood in Highland Hills and if they're still on our ass, let's go and check paper. Ya dig?" Devion said while peeping the scene with two of his own forty-fives tightly in his grip. Exiting off of Simpson Stuart and going toward their dad's grandmother's crib, they were still being followed, but by who was the question lodged into both of their minds. "Man, fuck all this shit, lil bro, I'm about to see what's happening, ya dig. These muthafuckas are being way too disrespectful and must don't love or value their life."

Pulling to a stop in front of Momma Faye's house, both of the brothers jumped out of the BMW 750 Li and headed straight to the car that had stopped behind them.

Momma Faye was an older woman in the neighborhood who had looked out for their father when he was a youngster running the streets. She had a way of telling you when you were wrong but never condemned anyone for their choices.

With guns in tow, Kevion was the first to notice that the two figures in the car were women. But coming up in the game and knowing that females could be the most ruthless and cold-hearted killers at times, he gripped his trigger even tighter and stood by his door to see what their next move was going to be.

Devion, who was a little bit more trigger happy than his brother, was wishing and hoping the women made the wrong move so he and his brother could get back to business. With a devilish grin, he aimed his two pistols, taunting the women to let them know that he was living like that and could give a fuck about leaving two bitches stinking if that's what the situation called for.

Getting impatient, Kevion or "KD" as the streets called him, was about to walk up and beat on the window with the butt of his gun. But right before he made his move, the door opened and the driver of the car stepped out.

"Look, homegirl, you better keep your hands where I can see them unless you want to turn your head into a drop top. Ya' dig?"

Kevion was strictly about his business, but he couldn't help but notice the beauty who stared back at him, unfazed and showing no fear.

With the chocolate skin complexion much like the beautiful Keisha in the movie Belly, she had long dreads that seemed to be freshly braided in a zigzag style to the back. She was tall, with long legs, and if Kevion had to guess, he'd say she was about six feet tall. Her outfit, a dark brown long leather skirt with a white belt, and a brown and white top was kicked off with some icy-white patent leather six-inch pumps. Aside from her thick in all the right places and toned body, she had seductive eyes that stared deep into Kevion's eyes.

She smiled, showing off her perfectly white teeth that had a small sparkling princess cut diamond placed in the center of all her visible front teeth. With a thick Jamaican accent, she said,

"Boi, put down dem der guns. I know ya' father, Derry Don did not teach you two ta treat ladies like dat."

Hearing her mention their father's name caught both of them off guard, but before Kevion could speak, Devion said,

"Bitch, I don't know who you are or how the fuck you know my pops, but you need to start explaining before I send a couple into yo' pretty lil face. While you at it, you need to tell ya' homegirl to get the fuck out befo' I check to see if ya' glass bulletproof, shawty!"

D-Mac, which was Devion's street name, was known for shooting first and to hell with the questions.

Kevion knew he needed to get the situation at hand under control.

"Hey D-Mac, go ahead and get the bitch out the car. Check her for guns and bring her next to her homegirl so they can decide their own fate. And if the shit ain't what they say it is, we gone tuck that ass in."

With a wave of her hand, the Jamaican chick signaled for the passenger to get out and to come stand by her before the overly anxious younger twin even had a chance to get to the door. When she stepped out of the car, the brothers saw that she had the height of a young teen, only about 5'4, no more than 5'5, and that was with six-inch heels. But she had the face and demeanor that was all business.

Dressed in an all-white designer dress that hugged her voluptuous hips, she showed off the high split running up the left side of her leg as she walked around the car in her open-toed gold with glitter shoes. By her looks, light brown golden skin and silky long wavy hair that hung loosely, stopping right above her apple bottom, the boys could tell she was Cuban or Puerto Rican.

"Damn! J-Lo ain't got shit on this bitch," Devion whispered to himself while steadily keeping his pistols trained on the two beautiful women.

She smiled, even in the face of death and Kevion noticed the same diamond wear in her grill. But it wasn't the diamonds that had his attention – it was the tattoo on her neck: A enormous "D" with #14 inside. It was the exact same tattoo that his mother had on her chest, over her heart. His glance moved to the other woman and he noticed that she had the same tattooed logo on her right hand between her thumb and pointer finger.

Knowing that mark represented their father, he wasn't sure what to think, so to get shit rolling, he asked,

"Who the fuck are y'all and why are you following us, shawty?"

The Cuban or whatever the hell she was, spoke up.

"Excuse us for being so rude, papi. We just missed you two at your mother's house, so we caught up with you on this side of town and were waiting' on y'all to stop, so we could introduce ourselves. My name is Cleopatra, and my beautiful friend here is Zolandria. We have specific instructions from your father to meet up with you two face to face. Although we've never met, we both know almost everything there is to know about the two of you since your dad is always talking and bragging about you."

Zolandria interjected, "Yeah, its Kevion dis and Devion dat. We even know you gave ya mom and dad a scare when you two were born prematurely at six months. However, you two are some soldiers and survived against all odds because you have heart and the fight of your father. Now I apologize if we scared ya or better yet, took ya out of your comfort zone by following you, but trust, we're not here to cause ya any harm, young kings. Your father is the king of our hearts and I know I can speak on Cleo's behalf because she has been down wit your dad a lil bit longer than I have. He has our trust, loyalty, and respect. So if you could, please lower ya weapons so dat we can get to the business at hand. If you don't believe us, you know ya dad has a cell phone in prison, you can call him up and see for yourself."

That beautiful Jamaican had said a mouthful that had the brothers' minds racing ninety-five miles per hour with thoughts and questions.

Kevion looked over at Devion and gave him a nod, signaling to put his guns away while at the same time, tucking his on top of his shirt, but into his waist for easy access, just in case.

"Man fuck dat, bro," Devion said. "How you gone trust these hoes and not call up Pops to make sho' these broads is who they say they are, my nigga?"

"Nigga! Put your fuckin' gun down and let's see what the fuck they gotta say. You see they got Dad's stamp on 'em, plus I know you saw that red beam flash across these bitches forehead. I know you know I came to this specific location for a reason, my nigga, because if anything goes left, the goons are going to be shooting diamonds out these hoes mouth, feel me?"

Devion was still skeptical, but knowing his niggas were inside the house they were in front of, he gave in to his brother. He tucked one of the guns behind his back and the other in his Sean John jeans pocket though he kept his hand on the handle.

“Devion, Papi, I told you to call your father if you think we are lying about who we say we are and that …”

Devion interrupted her, “Man fuck all that Senorita or Lil Cuban girl, my bro make a decision and Im'a ride with ‘em, ya dig? And the shit is vice versa, so let's cut all the excess small talk and get to what the fuck you want, cuz right now, you wasting our time, baby girl.”

“First of all, I'm Puerto Rican, but we came here to take you on a lil trip to meet someone of high importance to your father. Seeing that you two are following in his footsteps, your dad wants to set you up and get you out of the small time petty street life and get you two in the big boys' league. As far as I can see, you two aren't doing too bad, but if this is the life y'all are going to choose, you might as well go for the gusto, baby. Just having bail money and lawyer fees ain't gonna cut it. Even though your pops is going to take care of y'all regardless, it's time for the two of you to take the throne as the young princes that y'all are and uphold the family empire.”

“So let me get this straight, you two expect Devion and me to trust you two broads enough to go with y'all, who knows where, to meet who knows who, and everything is going to be straight just because you know a little info about us and you say you know our pops? Did I get all that right?”

“Look Papi, we can sit here and go back and forth on this until the sun goes down, but our jet awaits and like I said if you're scared...”

Kevion interrupted,”Yea I know, I know, call my dad, right? But word to the wise, don't you ever mention scared in the same sentence as our name, lady, and trying to play on my ego will get you choked, we clear on that, ma?"

"Crystal," replied Cleopatra.

Zolandria spoke up with her thick accent. "Look, why don't ya two go around da corner and drop yo car off at ya dad's grandmother's house? Miss. Jones has known us since way back when we met ya dad and once you see dat we ain't playing games, we can go catch our flight."

Devion whispered to Kevion, "Damn bro, these broads know G-Grams and everythang, what you think, bro?"

"If G-Grams knows them, the shit has to be straight because Pops don't just bring anybody around the fam, ya dig?" Kevion said and then turned back to the ladies. "Well, since y'all ladies know where my G-Grams stay, lead the way."

Showing off her deep dimples with a grin, Cleopatra said, "Come on."

The ladies returned to their car and the brothers did, too.

Before they drove off, Kevion's phone rang. Looking down at the screen, he saw that it was their dads trusted friend Curtis. "Hey, what's good C-Biscuit?" Kevion said, calling him by the name he was given by his friends.

"Shit, just making sure y'all lil niggas straight. You know I've been peep'n the play since y'all rolled on the block. What's going on with that anyway? Or do y'all have the situation under wraps?"

Curtis and their dad had been friends for years. They always looked out for one another like they were family. When

Derry Don went in for his "vacation" Curtis promised to look out for the twins.

"Naw C-Biscuit, we straight, but I appreciate you for looking out, though. I know that was one of y'all back there ready to put a peephole in them bitches' dome."

Curtis laughed.

Kevion continued, "We are about to roll over to G-Grams house and make sure everything is straight for real, though."

"Alright lil nigga, let me know what's good. You know where I am. Holla back."

# Chapter 2

**P**ulling up to their father's grandmother, their great-grandmother's house, Zolandria, and Cleopatra got out of their car, walked up the driveway and rang the doorbell. Kevion and Devion were coming up behind them when the door opened and their great-grandmother said,

"Hey girls, what brings you this way?"

Zolandria spoke up, "Well, ya know we are always checking up on ya, Miss Jones, but D's sons don't believe we know der father."

Their great-grandmother peeped out the door.

"Hey, great-grand's! What's this all about?"

"That's what we are trying to figure out, G-Grams! Devion and I were rolling when these two popped up out of nowhere talking like they've known us our whole life. I see dad's stamp on them and everything, but we had to come over here and find out for ourselves since they said they know you and all."

"Well yes, they have known both of you since you were born. All the way back to when you were both kicking and fighting over the last piece of chicken in your mom's stomach." Miss Jones chuckled.

"Well, how come me and Devion are just now seeing them then, G-Grams?"

"You have to ask your dad about that. I know they were around you two when you were babies, but they weren't around as much as y'all grew older. You know your dad. He has his reasons and you know how secretive and protective he is. Miss. Cleo here has been around, what twenty-four, twenty-five years?"

"Twenty-four Miss Jones," Cleopatra said.

Miss. Jones continued, "And Zolandria, I met her a year after that, which was a year before you two were born. It shouldn't be surprising that I took an extra liking to her, being that the first part of her name is exactly the same as my first name. Though I love 'em the same, especially because they are able to deal with your father and love him the way they do. I'm sure the next time you two go visit with him, he'll explain everything to you. Okay, baby?"

"Yes ma'am," the twins said in unison.

"Look, G-Grams, we gone leave the car here while we take a ride with them for a while. Do you need me or Devion to do anything before we leave?"

"No, I'm alright. You two just be careful."

Right before they made it to the front door their great-grandmother said, "Oh yes there's one very important thing I want to do before you all head out."

Devion let out a small sigh and under his breath said, "I know where this is going."

They all turned around and looked at Miss. Jones.

She looked at Devion and said, "I heard that boy! And you are right. I ain't never gonna change. I'm always going to keep my family covered in prayer. With all the knucklehead stuff you twins and your dad find yourself into, I've about worn my knees raw with prayer. You better believe it's only by the grace of God and the prayers of both your grandmother and me, that y'all are still here. We've been praying for you from the very first time we laid eyes on you. I remember when you were first born and they wheeled you past us on your way to the Neonatal ICU. Y'all were so small. We had never seen any babies that small in our lives. Your grandmother was so overcome with emotion she almost fainted right there in the hallway. I held her steady and immediately begin to call on the name of Jesus. We prayed the entire time you were in the hospital. I even put scriptures on your incubators to let the world know y'all were special gifts from God. So hush up and bow your heads."

The atmosphere in the house had changed instantly while listening to their great grandmother speak from her heart. They knew they were born under extremely dire circumstances and had been given a very slim chance to live, but every time they heard the story of their arrival from their mom, grandmomma and great-grandmomma, it always made them feel a certain kind of way. They had both concluded that the everlasting fight and determination to always win, in any situation, came from the battle they endured over the first year of their lives, to live despite the doubts of everyone in the medical profession.

Their great-grandmother closed her eyes and placed a hand on a shoulder on both twins. Zolandria and Cleopatra held hands.

"Dear Heavenly Father, I come to you as humbly as I know how. First I want to say Thank You for the many blessings you have bestowed on my family and me. Thank you for keeping us in spite of the many dangers, toils and snares of this wicked world. Heavenly Father I ask that you continue to watch over my great-grandson's. Go before them in any and every situation they may find themselves into. I pray that you keep your angels of protection around them at all times. I cancel any plan Satan has to destroy their lives and declare that grace and mercy shall follow them wherever they go. In the mighty name of Jesus I pray. Amen".

In unison, everyone said "Amen."

Turning to Cleopatra and Zolandria, she said, "And you ladies make sure you take care of my great-grandbabies."

Cleopatra and Zolandria both gave her a hug and planted a kiss on the opposite sides of her face before walking towards the front door.

Kevion and Devion both kissed their great-grandmother.

Kevion said "Thanks for the prayer G-Grams. We know you always got our backs."

"Yeah, thanks and we love you too Granny," Devion said with a devilish little grin.

"Now you know I don't go for that granny stuff boy!" Miss. Jones said with her hands on her hips.

"I may be saved, but I'm still the classiest great-grandmomma in Highland Hills. Don't get it twisted." She smiled and everyone burst out laughing.

"Okay G-Grams, we feel you," Devion replied. "My bad little lady. My bad."

Their great-grandmother walked them to the door and waved goodbye.

As the four got into Zolandria's car, Kevion called Curtis.

"Hey, C-Biscuit check it, we are about to take a trip right quick. Hopefully, in search for bigger and better dough. Everything is straight with that issue earlier. But I need you to call TK and JoJo for me and tell them to handle their spots for us until we get back. Let them know it's two whole chickens in the deep freezer in the basement in case they get hungry instead of buying fast food."

"Gotcha," Curtis said.

No one on the streets talked outright on the phone about business; they always spoke in code. Kevion knew Curtis understood what he'd just told him -- the cocaine was in the safe under the house in case TK and JoJo ran out before Kevion and Devion returned.

Kevion added, "We shouldn't be gone longer than a few days."

"Alright my nigga, I'ma call 'em up now and let 'em know what's good. Y'all lil niggas be safe and keep your heads on a swivel."

"You do the same and we'll hit you when we get back."

The moment Kevion hung up, Devion realized that neither he nor his brother had a change of underwear.

"Hey, we need to get some drawers and clothes befo' we up and vamp. Swang by the mall right quick, shawty," he said to Zolandria "I'm a grown nigga, but my nuts and ass I keep so fresh and so clean-clean," he added imitating the hit song from Outkast.

"Just sit back and relax fellas, we already got that taken care of," said Cleopatra.

Kevion asked, "So what's the story on y'all two? Y'all say y'all love my pops and shit, so what, y'all work for him or something?"

Cleopatra rolled her eyes and said, "What? You wanna know if we hoe for yo daddy? Is that what you're implying?"

"Yea, are y'all his hoes or what?" Kevion replied.

"I'll put it to you like this, whatever your dad, My Daddy, asks me or tells me to do, I'll do it no matter what. No questions asked. For one, he has always had my back and my best interest at heart. For two, his love is far greater than any other love I've ever felt. But most importantly, I truly wanna make and see him happy."

"Ya couldn't have said it any better, Cleo," Zolandria said. "Did dat answer ya question, sir?"

"Yea, that's what's up," Kevion said with a smirk on his face.

Zolandria said, "Look boi's, ya father wanted ta make sure dat whatever ya chose to do wit ya life was strictly ya decision and yours alone. He kept you from having ta see the street life or any of the business he was involved in. I know he taught ya certain lessons on life dat would have prepared you for any situation, whether you chose to be in the streets or da executive suites."

Cleopatra cut in, "Growing up in the hood, around dope sales and eventually meeting a much older woman who taught him and molded him in the game of Pimpin' and Dealing, your dad knows the effects the streets had on him. That is not the life he wanted for you. But seeing and hearing that you two have made up your minds to go down that path and become your own bosses out here in these wicked streets, he's ready to open up and share all of his secrets that helped him rise to the top of the game."

Kevion was thoughtful for a moment before he said, "So let me guess, you two are the first secret revealed to Devion and me, right? And if I'm not mistaken, I think you mentioned that our mother knows you as well."

"Correct and correct," Cleopatra said. "Listen, you know your father and mother love you two dearly and he just wants the best for you regardless of what decisions you make. He is always going to protect you any way he can, especially when he gets out in two years. Then, we will all be back together as we once were. Understand there are more family members, as far as other women go, but we've been around longer and have built up a certain level of trust with him, so that's why we met first or should I say again."

# Chapter 3

Exiting the highway off of I-20 and Hampton, Zolandria pulled onto an airstrip at Red Bird Airport. The entire airport was private and only private businesses or private jets were allowed to use it.

Devion said, "So I guess dis another one of his secrets, huh?"

Zolandria nor Cleopatra said a word. Zolandria showed the proper credentials to the security guard at the entrance and proceeded inside the gates toward hangar number 6. As they approached, the massive hangar doors opened for them to park inside. A midsize jet bearing the infamous trademark "D-#14" awaited inside ready for them to board.

Kevion tried to hide his surprise. *Damn Pops, you got it like that, huh?* He thought to himself. *I know you a hustling muthafucka, but damn, I didn't think you were getting cake like that old man.*

Devion didn't hold his thoughts or first impression. "Yo, that's my dad's right there or is y'all bullshitting me? Dat muthafucka there is the shit. Look at dis' shit, KD bro. How the fuck dad gon' hold out on a nigga like dat'? I bet moms knew about dis' shit, too. Oh shit, so this is how grandmom's be able to leave whenever she pleases, going from state to state doing her thang wit dat' interior decorating and shit."

"Yea, it's all starting to make sense to me too, bro. I always thought it was Uncle Cameron hooking her up since he played in the NFL," Kevion said, referring to their uncle's professional career as a linebacker for the 49'ers.

As they got out of the car, a man walked up to the trunk of the car and retrieved the ladies' bags and put them on the aircraft.

"How's everyone?" he asked. "Are you all ready for take-off?"

Cleopatra smiled and responded, "We're fine, Jonathan, how are you?"

"Blessed ma'am."

"Well, I would like you to meet…"

Jonathan interrupted before Cleopatra could finish, "This must be Kevion and if I'm not mistaken, that's Devion. Am I correct, young fellas?"

Devion looking perplexed, said, "Man, how you know which is which?"

As he led them onto the plane, Jonathan explained,

"Well, your father is always talking about his boys and showing me pictures whenever he gets new ones. I know who you are because even though you and Kevion are indeed identical, you wear your clothes a little bit more loosely than your brother there."

Devion chuckled. Jonathan was right. Unlike Kevion, who was much more business ready, sometimes even wearing tailor-made double breasted three piece suits, Devion was far more casual.

Devion nodded his head and said, "Right On."

Jonathan turned to Cleopatra and Zolandria. "Do you all need anything before I get this thing in the air? There's food in the fridge along with juice and soft drinks along with...."

"You got some Remy?" Devion spoke up.

"Yes sir, there's champagne and other liquors, including Remy Martin and the finest cigars for you, Mr. Devion. But please, allow me to get leveled before you move around for your safety. I'll let you know when it's safe to unbuckle your seat belts. Just sit back and enjoy the flight."

"Thank you, Jonathan," Cleopatra said, "I know we're in trusted hands."

Once the plane leveled and it was safe to move about, Devion retrieved two glasses, some ice, and a bottle of Remy Martin VSOP for him, and a bottle of Crown Royal for his brother since he knew his twin's drink of choice. He poured his brother's drink first, then his.

"Excuse me, sir, would you be so kind to pour a lady a glass of champagne? It should be some Cristal on ice," Cleopatra said.

"Pour me a glass of dat, if ya don't mind," Zolandria added.

"My bad, ladies, but ain't nothing wrong with you two bitches. Yo' legs and hands look like they work perfectly fine to me."

When Cleopatra and Zolandria both raised their eyebrows, Devion added, "Naw, I'm just fuckin' wit you, boo. I got you, ma." Devion smiled.

Pouring the drinks, Devion continued, "But yo', this plane is off tha' hook, shawty! Bro, it's a shower in the back wit beds and everythang in dis joint. Yo, pops doing it big. How he gon' keep dis shit from us like dat, bro? I can't wait to go see his ass and charge him up bout dis here."

"Yeah, alright bro, I gotta see that. You know pops don't give a damn because he locked up. That nigga will still beat the piss out of your ass if you come at him sideways."

"Nigga, you know I ain't gone even go at him like dat, but damn, he oughta let a nigga vent a lil bit for keepin' secrets and shit. I know he can give me some leeway and respect a nigga. Ya feel me? Then Devion turned to the ladies. "Miss Cleo, where we headed and how long dis flight gon be, ma?" Devion asked.

"The plane ride is three hours, but you'll see where we're going when we get there."

"So we still with the secrets, huh?" Kevion asked. "Damn, three hours! Shit, I'm glad I brought my shit with me; where are those cigars at again, ma?"

"Hey bro, roll up so I can calm my nerves," Devion said while handing his brother the ziplock bag filled with Kush weed. Then he pulled out three Cuban cigars from another bag and about seven grams of cocaine or as he liked to call it, "Dat Dust", and dumped some on a mirrored tray that he found on the plane's bar.

"Boi, do ya know what ya doing wit dat,' youngsta?" Zolandria said playfully.

"What? You wanna get down or you wanna talk shit out ya diamond crusted grill, lil girl?"

She flipped open the arm of the chair she was sitting in, pulled out a bag of dust of her own, and threw it on Devion's lap. "Dat right der, young man, I know for a fact is way betta than dat stepped on shit you got, lil nigga."

"Stepped on? You must don't know who you dealing wit, lil mamma. I fucks wit nothing but top of the line shit. Ya dig? From all my hoes, all the way down to tha' chinks dat do my toes. Ya' dig? You can best believe if it ain't tha' best, I pays no attention and stay on my quest. But from the looks of it, shawty, it looks like you got dat' good-good. But try dis out and let me know what's good."

Kevion fired up two blunts and passed one to his brother, before he reclined his chair back and allowed the Kush filled cigar to relax his mind.

Even though it looked like he remained in deep thought, Cleopatra broke his concentration when she asked,

"Kevion, why are you so quiet? It seems like you're a million miles away. I know you two haven't seen us since you were babies, but trust, you can talk to me about any and everything. You two are like my own and as far as I'm concerned, I have nothing but love for you."

When Kevion stayed quiet, she kept on, "I know we seem like strangers right now, but we have been there every step of the way. I felt great pain when we were told that we couldn't see you two until y'all got older, but we respected your father's wishes and understood why he did what he did."

Taking another pull on the blunt and inhaling deeply, Kevion looked in his brother's direction. He watched as Devion and Zolandria shared a blunt and snorted coke off the tray while laughing and engaging in conversation.

Turning back to Cleopatra, he stared directly into her green eyes before he said,

"Ma, I'm good, just wrapping my brain around all this. You know? I mean one minute we're driving, doing what we do. On a mission to get this paper and the next minute, we in the air, going I don't know where, with two ladies that's been knowing us since we were born. Only we have no recollection of them at all."

Cleopatra moved to the front of her seat to get a little closer to Kevion.

"Look, baby boy, I know it's a whole lot to comprehend at this moment, but eventually your dad was going to reunite all of us and give you the game to what's been going on all these years. But he just wanted to make sure you two chose your own destiny. I know for a fact that even though he didn't openly judge, he didn't agree with some of his associates who are in the game basically forcing their lifestyle upon their kids or other family members. He doesn't believe it's fair to insist that others take the same risk that someone else chooses to take themselves. Can you understand where he's coming from?"

"I feel that and I respect him for that. I'm also grateful that even though he made sure we didn't have to be in the streets, he never kept us blinded or hid us away from the streets either. He always treated us like men and prepared us for the world by dropping knowledge or game whenever he saw fit. He made sure we took care of business in school and he always made sure we honored our mother. When he left four years ago, me and Devion felt as though we had to hold shit down. We felt like we had some big ass shoes to fill. Ya feel me?"

Cleopatra shook her head to signal she understood.

"We were in our last semester of school and ready to graduate when he left to do his time in prison. Even though he told us not to worry about nothing, that everything was straight, I guess I just felt that I needed to take care of him and the family while he was on his mandated vacation. Since we knew we had kinfolk in the game who really have love and loyalty for us, it wasn't shit for us to get in where we fit in and start gettin' at this paper."

Kevion paused for a moment and glanced at his brother.

"Even though I wish Devion would have stuck with football. He was the real deal on that football field. The best wide receiver our school had ever seen. He had over six scholarship offers. But once Pops got locked up, he just stopped caring about sports and joined me in these streets. Ever since he bagged his first body, my bro has been on some "Fuck It" shit. He's gonna speak his mind regardless and give two fucks how a muthafucka feel."

"You muthafuckin right bout dat, bro!" Devion added while catching on to the last sentence his brother said. "Nigga don't be talkin' 'bout me ova there, homeboy like yo shit don't stank. O'le torture a nigga, mailing body parts to a nigga's T-Jones. Droppin niggas in acid and burying niggas in concrete, nigga!"

Kevion couldn't do nothing but give a devilish grin. But his brother knew when it came down to business or family, that Kevion was strictly business. He made sure he got his point across and understood to anyone that tried mistaking his kindness for weakness. Especially those who attempted to play him like he was some type of sucker, just because he didn't always use street slang and spoke proper English. This made some people question his street legitimacy, but he had a good way of showing them better than he could tell them.

Devion returned his attention to Zolandria, who was seated next to him obviously relaxed from the alcohol and narcotics they consumed.

"But yo', Miss Zolandria, what's happening wit you, tho, ma? I know you my ol' man's P.O.G.and err thang, but to be blunt, I wanna see what dat Jamaican pussy you workin' wit is all about. I've seen how you Jamaican bitches be moving on dem' videos and shit. I wonder if you can dance on dis' dick with dat' fat ass of yours. I bet you can't even take these two inches of hard dick."

Even though she was his father's Piece Of Game, Devion was still interested. He tried to play with her ego while making himself seem a little more mysterious.

"I know my pops ain't trip'n shawty, so what's happenin'? It ain't like I'm trying to take you from my pops or nuttin'. I just figure we keep it in the family. Ya dig?"

Zolandria was caught completely off guard by his words, but she was already feeling some attraction toward Devion. Even though she would never betray or leave her Daddy, their father, she was still human and was drawn to Devion's ruggedness, which was a trait that obviously ran in their family blood. She had also noticed that Devion must have worked on his body just as much as his father did. His athletic build made even more sense now that Kevion had mentioned his brother was one hell of a football player. His muscular arms, broad chest and stocky thighs, that she could see even in his loose fitting pants, made her visualize him jumping up and down, all around the bedroom, in her tight kitty kat.

She had to contain herself because she was starting to moisten her panties with the mere thought of taking Devion for a test ride.

"Yea, you probably right about him not minding," she said. "But at this moment, let's take care of business first, and I'll think about putting your ass to sleep while you're sucking on your thumb like the little boy you are. With your two inch ass," she said while taking another line straight to the dome.

Listening to their exchange, Cleopatra laughed while staring out of her window. The sky had darkened to night and she stared at the moon. At the same time, she thought about what her lover, her best friend, the only man that loved and respected her the way that she wanted, was doing at this very moment. She missed Derry Don so much. Even though she visited him on a regular basis and talked to him all the time, she was ready for him to walk out from behind those bars and back into her life full time. She knew that it was only a matter of time before they would be together again. Since there were no more secrets, as far as the boys were concerned, she wouldn't have to continue staying in a separate house from him any longer, once he was released from prison. With that thought, a smile formed on her face.

Kevion noticed her smiling and said, "What's got you over there showing all thirty-two, lil mama? Let me find out you over there thinking about my dad, shawty."

"That I am, Mr. Psychic. I'm just thinking about how I long for his touch and how beautiful things are going to be once he finally gets home."

With that, Kevion allowed her to remain in her thoughts while at the same time he turned his thoughts to how he was going to make his next move. He realized it would have to be better than his last move. He remembered some wise words his father used to say to him.

*Life is just like playing chess, my son. All of the pieces are before you and never hidden, but you have to learn to always stay three moves ahead of your opponent while protecting the kingdom, at the same time. Most importantly, always make sure that your pieces have protection and never, ever underestimate the pawns.*

Knowing that they still had a little ways to go on their flight, he made sure to tell Devion to be on point once they landed, by getting some rest and not getting too loaded. Before he reclined his chair and went to sleep himself, he took another pull on his blunt and downed the rest of the alcohol in his glass.

# Chapter 4

The Love Boys managed to get some much-needed rest during the flight. Their rest came to an end when they felt the bumpy landing of the plane. Forgetting where he was for a brief second, Kevion regained his focus and composure as he looked out the window and saw an unfamiliar landscape.

"Have you ever been to Afghanistan?" Cleopatra asked.

Before Kevion could answer, Devion said, "Awww hell naw! I know you didn't bring us to the Land of Bin Laden, shawty! Niggas be blowing they damn self up, so I know they don't give a flying fuck about my black ass. I'm glad I brought extra clips, cuz if I even see a muthafucka wit a backpack on, that's going to be too close fo' comfort. I'ma put two in his dome. Man, dis sum bullshit!

Letting Devion run off at the mouth, Cleopatra couldn't help but let out a loud laugh.

"Naw, I just wanted to see how you were going to respond, Papi. Actually we are in the beautiful country of Cuba."

Laughing as well, Kevion added, "You're a muthafucka, lil momma. Don't be giving my brother a heart attack like that!"

Once the jet came to a stop in the private hangar, they all exited the plane and approached a limousine that was awaiting them on the runway. Jonathan carried the ladies' bags and placed them inside the trunk of the limo.

"Thank you for getting us here safely, Mr. Jonathan. It looks like you could use some rest, darling," Cleopatra said.

"Yes, ma'am, I am a little bit tired, but luckily I prepared for this trip and got some rest beforehand."

"Well go ahead and make sure the plane is refueled before you leave. You will be staying at the usual hotel that we reserve for you. We called ahead to make sure the room would be ready and waiting for you. Your ride should be here shortly. If you need anything, you know the number."

"Yes ma'am, I do. Again, it was nice to finally meet you young fellas. Enjoy your stay in Cuba and I'll see you all later."

With that, the four of them got into the coldest all-white limo the Love Boys had ever seen. It was laced with all black leather seats with white custom stitching and exotic wood trim throughout with a stainless steel mirrored roof. The rear seats were captain's chairs with heat and massage controls. It was topped off with custom LED lighting, an onboard computer, WIFI and satellite TV.

The driver was a Spanish dude with a name tag that read Caja.

"Hola señor y señorita. Como Esta?"

Cleopatra responded, "Buenos Días Señor Caja. Muy bien, como esta papi?"

"Bien señorita."

"Are you ready to vámonos, papi?"

"Si senorita" the driver nodded his head.

After riding in silence for a few minutes, Cleopatra broke the silence and got the boy's attention.

"Listen up, who you are about to meet is a dear friend who is very important to your dad. They have been friends for close to twenty years and there isn't anything they wouldn't do for each other. They trust each other to the point that they both know whatever is asked will not put either of them in jeopardy because they want one another to be successful and prosperous in life. Trust me, Mr. Duran knows all about you two and he's been waiting to meet with the heirs of his dear friend for a very long time."

******************************

It took about ten minutes to arrive at their destination. The driver stopped in front of a large gate, rolled down his window and entered a code into a keypad. Within an instant, the massive gate opened and they traveled through. The sight of the huge Spanish-style home was something the Love Boys had seen on MTV Cribs.

Once inside, Kevion and Devion quickly overcame their thoughts of being impressed and put their guards up when they noticed there were men with assault rifles spread in various locations of the home. Even though they knew the men were posted on guard for security, the twins simultaneously pulled out their own pistols, checked their clips, and made sure there was one bullet in the head and their pistols were off safety.

Seeing them both react with caution, Cleopatra let out a small chuckle and assured them that they were safe and there was no need for them to be uneasy.

She said, "Trust me, if the guards were to shoot, it would strictly be to protect everyone that's part of this property."

Kevion quickly added, "Well if that's so, I need to be on point to help out and aid them in any way I can. You feel me? Because if he's as good of a friend as you say he is to my father, then my father would do the same."

"I feel you on dat, bro, but you already know how I roll. If they got guns and I got mine, I'll be damned if I get caught slip'n with my drawers around my ankles."

Kevion already knew what his brother thought because nine times out of ten they were thinking the same anyway. Kevion replied, "What's already understood…"

"Don't need to be explained," Devion finished the sentence.

"You already know." Damn! Dis look like some Don Corleone type shit K Dizzle! Look how big dis mufuck'n, shit is, I'ont know what ta' call dis' muthafucka! I'd feel like I was disrespecting dis mufucka if I called this a house," Devion said.

"Boi shut up and act like ya been 'round some money be'fo." Zolandria giggled.

"Naw shawty for real, I done been 'round and through some big houses befo' lil mama, but gawd damn it," Devion said, exaggerating the words.

About that time, a Cuban man who looked like he was in his early to mid-sixties entered the room. He was dressed in a white linen suit and wore a pair of brown Italian sandals. His shirt was unbuttoned revealing his upper body that showed signs of him maintaining some kind of workout, even though his chest was covered with salt and pepper hair. He also had war wounds on his stomach and chest that appeared to have come from gunshots or stab wounds.

"Please, please, come in," the Cuban said welcoming all four into the house. "I've been awaiting your arrival. How was the flight?"

"It was pleasant," Cleopatra said. Then, she turned to the twins. "Mr. Duran, I know you know all about them, but I would like to introduce you to Derry Don's sons. This here is Señor Kevion and this is Señor Devion; they're also known as The Love Boys, sir. You know their last name is Robinson, but this name just stuck with them since their mother's last name is Love."

With that introduction, the ladies excused themselves to lounge by the pool while the men talked business. Mr. Duran extended his hand to greet Kevion first and when he grabbed it, Kevion realized the old man still had a very firm grip. While looking directly into his eyes, Kevion said,

"It's a pleasure to meet you, Mr. Duran. I've been informed that you and my father are practically brothers."

"No, no, the pleasure is all mine, son. For a while now, I've wanted to see you boys again since you became young men."

"What chu mean again?" Devion said.

The old man said, "Well, Devion..."

"Wait, let me guess, you were also around and saw me and my brother when we were babies. Right?"

"That's exactly right, my boy. I was actually with your father at the hospital the day you were born. What was it? October 13th if I recall correctly. You two were so tiny being that you were born prematurely. You gave your father, mother and everyone a bit of a scare because the doctors had counted you two out. But look at you now. You two really have the hearts of your parents because they both have the hearts of lions." The old man took a cigar out and lit it while leading them both into one of his many living areas.

Not able to hold in his comments, Devion said, "Damn! Dis' crib is phat, Mr. Duran. I don't mean any disrespect, but how many banks you had to rob to be able to buy sum'n like dis?"

Letting out a single chuckle, Mr. Duran said, "Please just call me Duran or as your father calls me, D. But no, my boy, I'm not into the bank robbing business. I'd rather fill as many as I can. All it takes is being smart with your money and having patience. This type of house is something I've wanted for a long time, so I had it built from the ground."

Kevion interjected, "I appreciate you welcoming my brother and me into your home, and yes, it is a lovely one at that, but please if you don't mind, I'm still not sure of why we're here. I don't mean to come off rude, but I have no time to be on any kind of vacation. We must get back to our business in the states. We dropped everything and came on this trip on faith without actually tying up the business that we have going on back home."

"You two are just like your father," the old man said. "As you probably already know, your father speaks his mind, at will, and acts on impulses such as you, Devion. And when he needs to be calm, cool, collected and all about business, he is very much like you, Kevion. Your father and I have been making a lot of money for some time now. When I last spoke to him, he informed me that it was time for his boys to have the veil pulled from their eyes. Once he told me that, I already knew what path you two had taken. I've also heard a lot about you two. The way you conduct business and how you deal with problems back in the States. I also agree that it is time to elevate your game and leave the mere pennies behind. I'm only guessing, but about how much do you two generate a week? One, maybe two hundred grand a week? Between two and four keys a week?"

Kevion answered, "Yea, something like that. I'd say about two hundred and fifty thousand on the weeks of the first and the fifteenth, and about one hundred thousand in-between. You say it's just pennies, but we have the whole south side of Dallas under our control. Ain't nobody fuckin with us!"

Judging from Kevion's reply, it was evident his ego was shaken by the thought that what they were doing could be considered small fries.

"Please my boy, I don't mean to step on your pride at all, but I would think that you wouldn't mind earning between two and five million a week, getting out of that trap house, and minimizing the time you spend in the streets. Not only will you have, as you say, the hood on lock, but your entire city, then the entire state, and if you are as smart as I think you are, I have no doubt that you two would be the main suppliers from the third coast on to the west. Though I've seen families and friends torn apart because of greed, I feel that if you have an ounce of the same blood that's running through your father's veins that you believe family comes first, no matter what."

"You best believe dat. Without family and loyalty, you have nothing," Devion said. "And since I know how my father feels about friends, then you need not worry about me and my brother's loyalty, sir. Now don't get it twisted, I love what money can do. But I don't love it to the point where I'll sell my soul for it. I know I'm in these streets hustling and takin' souls, but dig, it's strictly business. Besides, these punk ass white folks wanna lock you up and shit fo' tryn' to make a mufuckin' dollar. So while dey at it, dey need to lock dey mufuckin' self up fo' bringin' da shit in the country on dey boats and planes. Ya dig?"

Mr. Duran nodded his head slowly and said, "Yea, everyone says that, but the problem is how are you going to lock up the very people who run the country? As long as they are making money, they are happy and they don't care whether you are free or not. They will make money if you are selling the narcotics or in the event that you are locked up, since the prisons are privatized and they own many of them, they will still make money. Either way, they are in a "win-win" situation. Your father and I will teach you how to handle your business so you won't have to worry about the government or the police. Your primary focus will be getting rid of the product."

"And what is the "product" you keep speaking of, Mr. Duran, I mean Duran?" Kevion asked. "And what are our roles or should I say, what is it that our father wants us to do exactly?"

"Well actually, my boy, it consists of two different products. Cocaine and Heroin are being used worldwide by millions of people. I don't have to tell you how lucrative the cocaine industry can be. Your father and I have invested a lot of money in coca and poppy fields. A little more than half a billion to be exact. So there's no middle man to worry about because the product is coming straight from our fields and directly from us. Since you are your father's sons, then basically those fields are as much yours as they are mine. Our plan is to earn more money and expand our areas as much as possible. Between your father and me, we generate a hundred million easily each month. But we have decided to start you off slow, to get your feet wet and give you the opportunity to get familiar with the other players in our organization. Since you have already made South Dallas a location for business, I know it wouldn't be any problem for you two to become the sole suppliers for the major players in the game in that area. Now what we need you to do as soon as you get back home is to first get your people out of those trap houses and off the streets. I know that's gonna be a challenge for some of your workers being that that's their only source of income. So pay them well for two to three weeks in advance, so they'll be comfortable until the ball gets rolling and they see some real cash flow."

Kevion said, "You want us to get everyone out of the trap? Does that mean to get rid of the houses as well?"

"No, not at all. We just need you to clean them up from the nickel and dime addict traffic. We solely want to turn those houses into stash spots and money counting spots. Understood?"

"That shouldn't be a problem," Kevion and Devion said in unison.

Then Devion said, "The quicker we get back home, the quicker we can shut everything down. It shouldn't take no more than a day or so to get rid of the product we have left and about a week till no more traffic is coming to our door."

So how long are we to remain here in Cuba, Mr. Duran?" Kevion asked. "Our father's pilot seemed tired and may not have the energy to fly us back so quickly, sir.

"That, my boy isn't a problem. If you two really want to leave tonight, I could have the pilot of my plane take you all back, and then he can return to Cuba on a commercial flight. However, you are more than welcome to stay in my guest house for the night. It will give us a little more time to talk business and get better acquainted. I know there's a lot I already know about you two, but I'm quite sure that's just the half of it."

"Yeah, we appreciate the offer and everything, but I think the sooner we get back home and take care of business, the better," Kevion replied.

"What's the rush, son? It's better to be careful so you won't have to be sorry later."

"There's no rush, and pardon me if I came off that way. I've always handled business with care, but thorough and aggressive at the same time. I'm basically just implying that I intend for business to go quite well, so our impression and reputation could speak for themselves."

Devion chimed in, "Check it, I'm down either way. I ain't got no problem staying in this big ass crib tonight. I bet the guest house is a good seven thousand square feet by it damn self!"

Duran chucked and said, "No, it's only six thousand square feet. Sorry to disappoint you. But it has its own gym, steam room, and hot tub to help y'all relax before getting back to business in Texas. It's also fully stocked with an array of new clothing, shoes and underwear in all styles and sizes."

"Damn!" Devion replied. "So Mr. Duran, answer this question for me if you can."

"Shoot, son."

"I remember back when I was in middle school when our mother would pick us up from school; some days we would go to this big ass house that really could have its own zip code, and she would say that it was one of our father's friend's house. She would always take in two big bags that looked as if they were stuffed with something, but when she came back, the bags would look empty. Whose house was that and what was in those bags?"

Letting out a slight, but loud chuckle, Duran said, "Well son, I'll put it to you this way, your mother will be changing her zip code soon. She's been waiting for your father to let her know when the time would be right to finally move into the home that she's been trying to hide from the two of you. Nine times out of ten, it was money she was taking to the house or filling her closet with some new clothes or shoes."

"Boy, dat's cold blooded. I knew it was sum'n up dat she wasn't tellin', but I just couldn't put my fanga on it. So what we gonna do KD? We staying or what?"

Kevion paused. Rubbed his hand over the waves on his head and said "Okay, cool. We will leave in the morning."

With that, Duran called out to one of his house staff "Lucinda, make sure the guest house is adequately prepared. We will have 4 guests tonight. Vámonos!"

Duran walked over to the fully stocked bar that was in the room and poured them each a shot of some aged and expensive liquor.

"To business, prosperity and health," and with a touch to all their glasses in a toast, they all downed the liquor, eagerly ready to get started on their new business venture at hand.

# Chapter 5

After a peaceful night of rest and a smooth flight back home, Kevion and Devion finally reached their car that they had left at their great-grandmother's house. Before they got out the car, Cleopatra said, "Now make sure as soon as you get everything shut down, you wait for an extra three to four days before you call to schedule your first shipment."

"No problem, ladies. I'll give you a call as soon as we get everything situated and under control. We are just counting on you to make sure everything goes according to plan once we shut down. We have your numbers so we will give you a call if we need anything, but I don't believe we will," Kevion said.

Cleopatra nodded and both she and Zolandria drove off.

Devion pulled out his Newports and lit one up. "Man, dis some crazy shit, bro. If dis shit be true, nigga, we gone have our own mills in a matter of months or better yet weeks, my nig. I know we don' touched a mill already, but I'm talkin' wit' an "S" on the end." Devion said.

"Yea bro, Pops was pretty smart with his money. It seems like all we have to do is handle business like we know how and make sure muthafuckas extinguish even the slightest idea of even thinking they want to fuck with us. Dig?"

"Like a shovel, bro," Devion said.

"Yo, let's swing by the house and them go by the spot and see what's happening with TK & JoJo. I told them we were going to hit them up when we got back, but since we shutting down shop anyways, we might as well give them a little time to sell as much as possible before we go see how much shit we got left."

*******************************

It was about 6:30 on a Friday night when the Love Boys pulled to one of their main spots for business in Oak Cliff. It was spring time, the middle of April, but the boys knew it was one of those nights when they generated a lot of money. It was the fifteenth. Not only was it payday for many people in the hood, but it was also the time of the month when people wanted to party, and not many of them worried about paying bills. Hell, most addicts didn't pay bills anyway, but the clientele the Love Boys commonly encountered were mainly smokers and not the lawn mower, copper pipe stealing, cluckers that only came for nickel and dimes.

The twins knew the best way to keep their spot off the radar was to sell big. Not only did the product move faster that way, but it also kept traffic to a minimum and nobody showed up without calling and placing an order first.

When the brothers pulled up, they noticed a couple of familiar customers who looked like they were getting back into their car and leaving.

"Looks like business is rolling as usual, KD," Devion said, as the brothers got out of the car and walked toward the door.

Kevion grinned and said, "I got twenty racks that these boys damn near put a bullet through the door when we get to knocking on the mufucka."

"I ain't fuckin wit dat, bro. You know just as I know JoJo stay ready to send somebody to an early grave, shit, I'll bet on Tony Romo's ass befo' I bet against that crazy ass nigga. What I look like Willie Foo Foo or somethin'?" Devion replied laughing.

"Aww nigga, you scared to lose a lil change, bro?"

"Call it what you wanna, nigga, but go find yourself a dummy. I don't bet 'less I know I'ma be counting someone else's paper in with my paper. Don't waste your time trying to play on my ego, kid. You know how I get down, lil nigga. Better yet, why don't you be the one to knock?"

Kevion accepted his brothers' challenge and banged on the door. Almost instantaneously they heard JoJo's voice.

"It betta be the mufuckin' man hisself wit a hundred mill, the way you out 'chea knockin'. If not, somebody 'bout to get made famous and put on a T-shirt! Who the fuck is it?"

"Yo' crazy ass nigga, who the fuck you think it is?" Kevion yelled back.

Opening the door with his gun in the other hand, JoJo said, "Aww, what's up, young G's? When the fuck y'all get back?"

"What's happening, cuz?" Devion said. "We just got back. What you know good?"

"Shit ain't, shit. You know we holdin' dis mufucka down till' y'all got back to get at dis chedda. But fuck, I thought you woulda hit us up once y'all touched down. Hell, I thought y'all was least gon' be gone for tha weekend. Shit, we still got half a key left."

"Naw, don't worry about that, kinfolk, we needed to hurry up and swang through here and bless y'all with the jewels that's been laid upon us," Kevion said.

"So what's up, lil cuz? Everything go straight on the trip or what?" JoJo asked.

"Yea, the trip was cool," Kevion said.

"Man, our pops is on some otha level shit, tho," Devion said. "Me and KD just found out he been keeping a whole lotta shit from us. Right up unda our noses and shit."

"What makes matters worse, hell our Grand T's and everybody been doing the same shit, ya dig."

"What you talking about, lil cuz?" JoJo asked.

Kevion cut in, "Listen, I'll put it to you like this, the hustling and money we've been making is going to seem like only a few dollars once we get situated and start fuckin' with basically my pops best friend who we met over in Cuba. You feel me?"

"He and Pops been getting at each other for a long time and now basically our product is going to be coming directly from the fields they already have set up."

"Yea, nigga, we about to step dis mufucka up and touch some real doe," Devion added.

"Y'all lil niggas lying! Why y'all frontin on us like dat?" JoJo exclaimed.

"Frontin? Nigga, you already know I ain't one of dem cash money niggas and I don't do no frontin' fam. Not only is we finna have tha coke game on lock, but we gon' have Boo-Coo Boy wit it," Devion said, referring to Heroin.

"Look, we need all of our workers to help us get rid of the last lil shit we have left, so we can shut down shop," Kevion added.

"All of 'em?" JoJo said.

"The three spots we have, we are going to turn them into stash spots. It's not going to be anymore trap'n and all that dumb, petty, small time shit will be in the past," Kevion explained with seriousness written all over his face.

"After dis, we going straight FED, niggas," Devion said.

Kevion continued, "Call up Lil Noah and the rest of the crew and see what they workin' with. Tell them to get rid of the product ASAP. Better yet, let them know it's about to be "buy two, get two free," so everything can be gone by the end of the weekend."

JoJo pulled out his phone to relay the message. "Y'all ain't bullshitting, huh?"JoJo said.

"Like my boy Trinidad James said, if you don't believe me, just watch," Kevion said.

JoJo laughed while the classic album by Young Jeezy, Thug Motivation, pumped through the speakers.

TK and JoJo were not only the Love Boys cousins, but they were their closest trusted friends. They had always been tight despite the decade age difference. Since their fathers were extremely close, they made sure they were always around each other growing up. Their father, Artis, had long left the thuggin ways of the streets, but they had decided to stay around as protectors for their younger cousins out of love and respect once they decided to get into the dope game.

After they informed their most loyal customers and got the word out on the street about the "buy two get two free" deal, their phones started to ring as if they were conducting a telethon. The crew damn near got rid of the rest of the coke that night, but they were sure to have moved all of it by the next day.

The Love Boys had not contacted their mother to see if she had moved into the huge house they remembered seeing years earlier. But as soon as they got rid of the coke, they were going to visit her and see what other secrets were bound to appear.

Saturday came and went, and just like they anticipated, with the word out on the streets, it was even busier than the day before. With practically no sleep, the brothers were still energized and motivated by thoughts of the income bracket they were about to leap into.

Sitting in the living room putting money in a medium sized duffle bag Kevion said,

"Hey, JoJo, I appreciate you and the rest of the crew for staying on the clock with us and helping by looking out the way y'all did. But look, all we have to do now is shut down shop and let everything die down until we get the first shipment. After that, the niggas we were getting product from can start getting their shit from us."

Kevion turned to TK, JoJo's brother and said, "Yo, call up Lil Noah because I know his hustling ass has gotten rid of all his product over at his spot. Tell him I said to get all the money together and meet us at the safe house. We are going to count all this loot up together and don't worry, I'm going to make sure everybody will be straight for the rest of the month".

"Nigga, we fam," TK said. "I already know yo' word is bond, feel me? So if you say a bigger and better plan is in play and gon' be good fo' all of us, then I already know tha shit is stamped and sealed. I'm cool on bread, so whatever you was gonna hit me off with just throw it in the safe fo' a rainy day fo' me.

Devion looked at TK and said, "You still ain't understanding Negro. What's coming, next is gon' be a different kind of rainy day. Nigga, we gon' be like the King of Zumunda off Coming to America kinfolk. Instead of rose petals being thrown at our feet, it will be nothing but the Benjamin's baby." Devion held out his hand to give TK a fist bump.

They all knew Devion never blew smoke up their asses or talked just to be talking.

"Alright fam, count us in. Just let us know what we are doing next."

******************************

Followed by JoJo and TK, the Love Boys pulled up to the safe house to see Noah's powder blue Mercedes Benz SUV already parked in the garage.

"Noah, don't be bullshitting, bro. Dat nigga 'bout tha dolla. My nigga stays on top of his business," Devion told Kevion.

"Yea bro, he's a real thoroughbred, cut from the same cloth we were cut from. He always had Pops' back as far as I can remember and the nigga stays loyal to the family," Kevion replied.

Grabbing the duffel bags full of money, they all exited their cars and went into the house through the door inside of the garage.

"What's up, fam?" Noah greeted them, sitting at the bar with a bottle of Hennessey and a blunt in hand.

"What's good, fam?" Devion shot back as they all threw a duffel bag onto the table that already had Noah's two bags on it.

Noah said, "Why the fuck we been giving away all dis mufuckin' dope? You know I don't like missing out on no paper, bro. Fuck, I don't care how rich I get, I'ma still squeeze a dolla out of a mufuckin' penny."

"I feel you on that," Devion said, "but check this, we gotta shut down shop at the trap, ya dig. Pour me up a shot of that Hen and pass the blunt. Check it, you already know we took a flight to Cuba and shit, and while we was out there, we met up with a nigga named Duran. Well check this shit out, he been partners with our Pops for a minute now, and they been makin' major moves on the low. I'm talking about, they invested their bread in their own coca and poppy fields, ya dig? Nigga, we been getting coke from these otha niggas, getting hit all upside our heads fo' tha shit, and we basically got our own fields to get tha shit from."

"Hold up! Hold up! Hold up!" Noah said. "You mean to tell me that we finna start making keys and shit our damn selves?"

"Yea, that's the next move bro." Devion replied.

"But check, we ain't neva fucked with dat boy, so how we gon' move dat shit if we don't even know how to fuck with it on dat level?" Noah asked referring to the addition of Heroin to their products.

Devion took a drag off his blunt and said, "Check, Duran said that he's going to plug us in with some players dat fuck with it in the D. So I figure once our name start to ring bells, shit, we ain't gon' have to look too far cuz mufuckas gone be looking fo' us, ya dig? Plus dem hoes ova in South Dino been making major moves they self, fuckin' wit it, and you know tha best customers been dem damn females off the rip."

"So look," Kevion interjected, "All we have to do is shut down the shop, get off the radar and wait for the first shipment, then pop back on the muthafuckin' scene, Jack! And when we pop back up, we won't be the one buying birds, we will be supplying them."

Noah took a pull on his blunt while thinking about everything that had just been laid upon him and a huge grin spread across his face with all of those dollar signs dancing around in his head and in front of his eyes.

"Yea, that's the same way we felt when the shit hit the fan," Kevion said. "Devion, TK, JoJo, and Noah, grab a bag and let's count this dough. The sooner we get through, the sooner we can break y'all off a nice chunk of change. Then we can board up the two spots so mufuckas will think we dropped from the radar. Besides, we need to go holla at moms and figure out the rest of this puzzle.

Four hours later and two hundred and fifty thousand dollars richer, they were through counting money.

"Man, even with all these paper cuts and finger cramps, I could never get tired of counting chedda," JoJo said.

"I feel you on that, big cuz, and I hope it's like you said, because the way I'm thinking, we are gonna' be counting rooms of doe like my nigga off "Blow." Now that nigga had paper cuz. He did stack some paper, but look where he at now. Locked up and been there for a nice lil minute now. That's something I don't want us to have to go through. Now, we already know the risk we take and death is often part of that risk, too. We have to stay smart, double and triple check everybody we fuck with; and then, we have to stay strapped at all times," Kevion advised.

"Nigga, I don't even go to the church without dat piece on me," TK said. "And you know JoJo crazy ass even got a pistol by his toilet and another in the muthafuckin' shower."

"Yea, I already know, I think that's where my brother picked that shit up from," Kevion said.

"You mufuckin' right," Devion said smiling. "Shit, niggas betta ask fo' they even make a sandwich in my house. Put ya hand in the wrong bread bag, and fuck around and pull out some nubs."

Laughing Noah said, "Hold up, bro, I know you ain't saying…"

Devion cut him off, "You mufuckin' right, nigga. I got the 380 in the dummy bread sack nigga."

"You are one crazy paranoid mufucka', lil bro."

"Call it what you wanna, mufucka; run up on me, nigga gon' come up missing," Devion said matter-of-factly with a scowl on his face.

"Alright, check it out, a hundred fifty racks up in the safe and everybody grab twenty a piece," Kevion said. "Hey D-mac, roll up another Kush blunt and let's take a minute out to just relax for a second because when the play go in motion, you already know it's gone be strictly business, all work, and no play. Just seeing D's house out in Cuba put enough motivation in me to get at this paper full throttle."

# Chapter 6

"Hey baby, whats up?" Brandie said when she answered her phone and recognized the voice of her oldest twin son, Kevion.

To the Love Boys, she was just their beautiful mother, but to Dante' or as everybody called him Derry Don, she was much more. To him, she was beautiful all the way around, through and out. She was a 5'5 caramel complexion sexy muthafucka! She had light brown eyes, barely weighed one hundred pounds, with a nice round fat ass that he loved to get a handful of or smack from time to time just to see it jiggle. Although she portrayed herself to be a sweet, loving woman when she had to be or needed to be, she was his complete equal, straight gangsta.

"You tell me what's up, Momma," Kevion said back into the phone as he drove down the highway.

"Where you at, T-Jones?" he asked her.

"I'm at the house, why?"

"Which one?" Kevion replied.

"The one I've been preparing for you two for a very long time," she said with a smile. "I know Duran told y'all everything. He called and told me that the two of you flew to Cuba and met him. Do you remember how to get to the house we used to visit each week a few years back?"

"Not exactly, but I know it's out in McKinney where Grand T lives. Right?"

"Yea, just come like you are going to her house and call me when you get to McDonald's over there on Ranch Parkway. I'll meet you."

"Alright. We should be there in the next forty-five minutes, Momma T."

"Okay, baby. I'll see you soon."

"Oh, hey, did you go see dad yesterday?" Kevion asked.

"Yes, I did. He thought that you and your brother were going to come since you made it back from seeing Duran, but the more he thought about it, he understood that you probably had a lot of business to tend to. He told me to tell y'all to make sure you come on the next visit so he could talk to you face to face. Alright baby?"

"Yes, ma'am. I'll call you when we get there, see you shortly."

After hanging up from her, they drove the rest of the way in silence, both contained in their own thoughts. They finally met up with their mother at the McDonald's and followed her to what seemed like the boondocks. They recalled the path and remembered all the trees that surrounded the land.

They finally pulled up to the house that they remembered from their early teens, and even though it wasn't as big as Duran's, it was just as extravagant. And that was just looking at it from the outside.

They got out of their car and embraced their mother in a group hug, each planting a kiss on both sides of her jaw, something they got from seeing their dad and Uncle Cameron do to their mother all the time.

"Hey babies, long time no see," she said after she stepped back from their kiss.

"Momma, it's only been a few days since we saw you last," Devion said.

"Yea I know, but any time away from y'all is too long for me. Come on in, let me show you our new home."

When they followed her inside, Devion said, "Daaaammn!!! I mean dang!" But he didn't change his slip-up fast enough and she gave him a slight punch in his stomach for cursing in her presence.

Kevion looked around at all the custom features of the home. Marble floor in the entry and hardwood flooring in other areas. A winding staircase and a kitchen with granite countertops and the largest island he had ever seen in a house.

"This is a nice house, T-Jones. How were you able to keep this away from us all this time? I mean, didn't you want to raise us up here?" Kevion asked.

"Of course I did, and if it were up to me, I would have. But you know your father. I can't tell him anything about raising his boys. I might be able to win an argument a time or two or get away on some things, but when it comes to you two, once he says what he says, you might as well just let it be."

The twins shook their heads, smiled and thought *Yep, that's Pops.*

Brandie continued "He wanted you two to grow up here as well, but even though he provided you with all you wanted and needed, he knew if you two were here growing up and around all of his associates that you would be choosing the path you chose because of him and the glamour you had been exposed to."

"Yea, he probably right," Devion said.

"So is there anything else we don't know about?" Kevion asked.

"Well there is one thing you don't know about," she said.

"And that is?" Devion asked.

"Tell me, do I look any different to you two?"

Kevion and Devion looked at their mother and when she raised her shirt to reveal a slight bulge in her stomach, at the same time they said, "What is that? I know it ain't...."

"Yep, I'm expecting another baby!" she said excitedly.

"How is that possible?" Kevion asked. "And I know you ain't stepping out on Pops, are you?"

He didn't give her time to answer and continued, "I mean I noticed you have been eating a lot and I saw that you've been gaining weight here and there. So whose is it?"

"Silly lil boy, it's your father's. You know I love that man too much and there will be no other man for me."

"But how? He's been locked up for almost two years now, Momma." Kevion asked with a look of puzzlement.

"Well, you already know he has pull with the warden and guards where he is, so a few months ago he paid for us to have a "special visit."

Kevion and Devion started to smile, and then Kevion asked, "So what are we gaining. A brother or sister?"

"I don't know, we'll all find out once it gets here. I knew you two were boys before y'all were born, but this one, I want to be a surprise."

"Man, I hope we have another brother," Devion said.

"A brother? No, I hope I'm having a girl this time. I've had enough of boys after raising you two hard heads."

"It ain't like you are an angel, Momma," Devion said under his breath.

Brandie playfully thumped Devion on his forehead and said, "Yes I am," while showing off her devilish diamond grill. She sported the same kind that Cleopatra and Zolandria had except her diamonds were canary yellow.

"Yeah, okay Mom, whatever you say, T-Jones," Kevion said while laughing.

"Before you even ask, your grandmothers already know and they are both as thrilled as we are. Now look boys, you know I I love the both of you very much and I'll always have your back in whatever y'all do. I just want you two to be careful and make smart decisions so you two can be alive and free well into your older years."

"I know Momma and we will," Devion said.

"So what are y'all going to do with the old place? Sell it?" Kevion asked.

"No. We're going to give it to my brother and his family. That place has too many memories for us to just let it go. You two grew up there and not only that, you were conceived there as well. Hell, that's where I met your father's hustling ass. I remember that day like it was yesterday. I was driving into my community; it was one of those hot sunny days. Your father was strolling along the sidewalk when he spotted me and waved me down. I stopped to see what he wanted and after he had checked me out to make sure I wasn't the police, that Negro asked if I smoked weed. I was like yea, why? Then he told me to take down his number and hit him up when I needed some. From that encounter, we started kicking it and a year later, you two were placed in my womb."

She paused and shook her head.

"God! How much I miss that man and can't wait for his sexy black ass to come home. Anyway let me get off that before I start crying and all that shit. He loves you boys very much and only wanted to provide the best for you and allow you two to make your own decisions in the life you chose. You two make sure y'all look out for each other in those streets. Even though I don't want y'all out there, I can only give you advice to keep you ahead of the game. Trust, I've been there, especially once I met your father, and just watching him, I've learned alot. Your dad is younger than me, but he's older and wiser beyond his years."

"Alright momma, you know we got each other's back out here so don't worry about that," Kevion said. "We have to make a move to go tie up loose ends so we'll be ready when it's time to holla at Mr. Duran, okay?"

She nodded.

"You need anything before we leave?" Devion asked.

"No baby, I'm all right, y'all go on and handle what you need to do, but make sure y'all aren't busy when I go visit your father next weekend, okay?"

"Alright," Kevion said.

"Y'all sure y'all want us to come? I don' wanna be interrupting y'all grove thang y'all got going on up there in the penitentiary," Devion said.

"Boy shut up and get on out of here. Trust me you will not be getting invited when it's our time."

"Awww I don't wanna hear all that, you coulda kept that," Devion said, as he pretended to cover his ears.

"Well, you shouldn't have asked then, smart ass."

"We'll call you later on, Momma."

Then together, both boys said, "Love you."

"Love you too, boys."

Leaving the house and getting back onto the freeway heading south, Devion turned the volume up once he heard the lyrics to one of his father's favorite rappers, which was now one of his, DMX.

*One mo road to cross, one mo risk to take, gotta live my life like it's one more move to make….* Kevion and Devion bobbed their heads and sang along, feeling that this song pertained to them, especially since they were waist deep in the game. And now, they had even bigger plans to get in even deeper.

"Yo' dis mufucka keeps it 100 G," Devion said. "I can't believe my dog fell off like that. Nigga went from making mills off records to stealing cars and smoking crack and shit."

"Yeah, that was some shit, bro," Kevion added.

"Yo take me to the pad so I can jump fresh and get my whip," Devion said.

"Yeah, I need to jump in the shower too. I know I ain't hit the water since before we left. Nigga been on a nonstop hustle getting shit straight. I'm starting to smell myself," Kevion said.

"Yea, you'za funky mufucka, bro. Crack a window in dis joint; you killing me ova here," Devion said laughing.

"Nigga, you act like your shit don't stank; you ain't hit no water in a minute either, fam."

"Negro, I already know that; why you think I'm tryin' ta get there so fast?" Devion said.

"Fo' sho," is all Kevion shot back. "But check it, I'm going to hit Loco up and go holla at him and let him know what the business is later on tonight. He's been our boy since grade school and is like family. He has always been loyal and a reliable supplier, so if and when we take off to another level, we are going to make sure he is straight because he has always looked out for us, ya dig?" Kevion said.

"You already know, bro. Tell my nigga Loco I said what's up for me. When you get through come holla at me over at Club X. After I finish going by the spots to make sho they look deserted and abandoned, I'ma scoop up some drank and head ova to the club. My mind be relaxed mo' around naked hoes rather than niggas in the streets. I'ma cop you some Henny while I'm at it and put it on ice," Devion said.

"That's a bet, bro. Yeah grab up seven grams of Kush for me too, and some Garcia y' Vegas cigars, ya dig?"

"Like a shovel," Devion said.

When they reached I-635, they went East and headed toward Garland where they shared a two bedroom, two bath townhome. They arrived, and jumped out of the car and once inside, they went directly into their separate bedrooms.

"Yo! Throw one of dem pizza joints in the oven so we can put sum'n on our stomachs, bro," Devion said. "My shit is touchin' my back.

"Fuck I look like? Your maid or something?" Kevion shot back.

"Man you be on some nigga take ya tampon out ya ass, patna!"

"I got you, bro," Kevion said.

After throwing the pizza in the oven, Kevion went into his room which was downstairs and went in his closet where all his clothes were lined up. They'd just gotten a lot of clothes from the cleaners, so neither one had to iron anything.

Since Devion had been given a head start, he had already picked out his attire for the evening. He decided on a black and gold True Religion outfit. The base of the shirt and jeans were black with gold design logos running down both the back of the jeans and all through the shirt. He chose a pair of Gucci shoes to complete the look. He chose a pair of gold nugget dollar sign earrings, sprinkled with crushed diamonds to accompany the half karat diamond studs; he always wore, along with a gold and diamond 'D' to hang on a chain around his neck. For the finishing touch, he pulled two diamond crusted pinky rings from his jewelry box to bring an air of class to the entire ensemble.

*Yea, nigga gon' be the flyest tonight*, he thought to himself while putting in a CD by the artist Sugar Free, and quickly went to the track titled "On My Way." He threw a pair of Gucci briefs on the bed along with matching Gucci socks with a black t-shirt and proceeded to the shower.

Just before jumping in the shower, Kevion decided to dress down from his usual business like attire. He settled on a blue and white Polo shirt, some starched down blue Polo jeans and some all-white and blue Adidas shell toed shoes. To accentuate the outfit he pulled out a platinum diamond encrusted cross chain with a platinum diamond bezel Rolex, platinum diamond-encrusted hoops for his ear lobes and a diamond band to be worn on his right ring finger. The ring symbolized that he was married. But this marriage was a little different. He was not married to a woman, "The Game" was his bride.

Since Devion was the first to get out the shower, he ran downstairs and pulled the pizza out of the oven, wanting to give it some time to cool. Then, he went back up to his room and dressed.

After they had finished dressing, they each grabbed half a pizza along with a Miller High Life. After washing down his last slice of pizza with a swig of beer, Devion said,

"I'm about to be out, KD. It's almost 8:30; so I'ma git up to the liquor store before it closes down on a nigga. Tell my nigga Loco what I said and hit me up in the club later on. I should be there by 10:30 or 11 o'clock."

"That's a bet. And make sure ain't nobody been fuckin' with the spots and that they all sealed up bro. You have your pistols?" Kevion asked.

"Shit, I'll forget my nuts before I fo'get my babies, bro."

"Alright, just checking, bro, clips full?" Kevion asked.

"Yea, along with the other two," Devion said slyly.

"Alright, be careful out there, bro, and hit me up if you need me."

"No doubt, fam."

After dapping each other up, Devion went out and got into his pearl-white, two-door Audi A6 and burned off.

Kevion finished dressing and topped it off by spraying on the intoxicating scent of Paris Hilton for Men. He jumped into the pine forest green colored BMW 750 and immediately called their friend and longtime supplier, Loco to tell him he was on his way over.

"Damn lil, nigga, so soon?" Loco asked while talking in code over the phone. "Y'all lil niggas just left a few days ago."

Chuckling, Kevion said, "No, it's nothing like that fam. I need to come holla at you, though and put you on some changes to the game. I'll be there in about fifteen minutes."

"Yea, okay," Loco said before they both hung up.

□

# Chapter 7

Devion made it to the liquor store before it closed and was able to get their drink of choice. After checking on the spots and sitting at both of them for about thirty minutes a piece, he went and purchased the Kush weed to go along with the bag of powder he had for his personal use. Once he confirmed everything was in place, he headed to the upscale strip joint.

Devion was already inside the well-known **Club X** when Kevion arrived. He found him at the back corner table upstairs where all the main strippers were. Sitting at the table with about a gram of cocaine on a tray with both of their favorite drinks on top with a bucket of ice and two glasses, Devion got up and greeted his brother with a shake/hug.

"What's tha word, bro? What my nigga Loco got going?" Devion asked.

"Everything is straight with Loco. I filled him in on a "need to know basis" until we confirm everything on our end. I informed him of the new cocaine connection but didn't tell him that we are going to be the supplier. I think we need to keep him in the dark about that just in case shit don't play out like it supposed to. Did you check on our spots? Is everything locked down?" Kevion replied.

"Yea, we good. Both tha spots look like a ghost town and shit. Dem dope fiend niggas who are always coming around wanting to do anything they can to stay in our good graces, did they thang and boarded up the windows real good. Everythang is locked down tight, bro."

"Alright, we need to hit Duran up tomorrow to let him know everything is straight on our end and that we'll be ready by next week." Looking down at the table, Kevion asked, "Is that Kush or what?"

"Here, fire one up. I already got two blunts rolled up, bro. You gotta po' up yo own troubles, though," Devion said.

Taking a line straight to the dome, Devion sat back, took a sip of his Remy Martin straight from the bottle when the hit song from Lil Wayne poured though the speakers: My Leather so soft.

As soon as the song rang through the club, every stage and pole was covered by sexy, seductive dancers, with the rest of the women scouring the floor in search of tricks who wanted lap dances or special sexual encounters that could be given in the back rooms. Since most of the dancers knew the Love Boys, they already knew that the twins were strictly business and weren't the type to be tricking money off with them. So when the strippers passed, they just greeted them, hugged them, and even planted kisses on their cheeks while whispering seductive words in their ears. Just about all of the women wanted to be in their company, and some even wanted to be their lady. But the women knew that even if they were lucky enough to be chosen by them, it would be nothing but a quick 'Wham, bam, thank you ma'am' type of fling.

One of the new girls who didn't know the brothers was impressed by them. She was taken with the ice they sported, and the way they carried themselves.

As she approached their table, Devion had his head in his tray. She leaned over and whispered in his ear,

"For the right price, you can get this pussy all night long, Papi."

Devion rose up, thinking that was one of the girls he knew fucking with him; but when he saw the unfamiliar face of the tall, yellow-boned female whose voluptuous breasts, with perky fat brown nipples, were exposed, he sized her up for a second.

*Damn, dis bitch could get it and she might be on my agenda for the night*, he thought to himself. He looked at her with menacing eyes, cracked a devilish grin, then reached into his pockets and pulled out two stacks of money that were so thick, they couldn't be folded, and placed them on the table.

Her eyes widened as she thought, *Damn this might be pay night.*

But then, Devion busted her train of thought and burst her bubble at the same time. "Pussy is sweet and so is honey, but I'd rather choke my chicken and save my money." Making himself another line as he basically dismissed the rather beautiful dancer, she did nothing but look at him, but realized his response caused her to like this mysterious man even more.

She thought, *Damn, ain't nobody turned me down like that before. He might get this ass for free.*

She turned and walked away with a smile on her face in search of another sucker.

When Kevion caught her smile, he told Devion, "I don't know what you told shawty, but it got her cheesing from ear to ear."

"Word?" Devion asked. "Aww shit, she just might be on the menu for the night since she digging my swag like dat."

"Yea, lil momma was right, bro, with her pretty ass titties and fat ass. I didn't see a pimple on her."

The brothers continued to enjoy the rest of their drinks while smoking the potent weed. Right before the club closed, Kevion had already made plans with a regular female who chose him a while back named Hershey. Hershey was a chocolate-toned shawty who was 5'5 in height with a slim waistline. She had nice, voluptuous breasts with an apple behind and light brown eyes. They agreed to meet back at Kevion and Devion's apartment to continue their night. Since she was proven to be loyal and had been breaking bread with KD, he didn't have a problem showing her where he laid his head. One thing about the Love Boys – they never trusted and most importantly never showed anyone where they slept. But Hershey was cool so Kevion made an exception to the rule.

When they were getting ready to leave, the same yellow-boned woman that approached Devion earlier came back. Now dressed, she dropped the bag of money she earned from the night into Devion's lap and looked him deep into his eyes.

"Bitch! You reckless eyeballin a pimp," Devion spat at her, just to let her know what she was getting herself into.

All she said was, "I know Daddy and I chose you. My name is Honey and I wanna make you rich by being your bitch."

Grabbing the large bag of money, he took the bills out, and without even counting, he stuffed the money in his pocket. Looking over at his brother, he dapped him up and said, "I'll be at tha crib in the morning, bro."

Kevion nodded to him and watched as his brother got up to leave.

"Come on, bitch, let's go," was all Devion said to Honey.

# Chapter 8

Honey had driven to the club in her stylish Honda Civic, so she followed Devion to his regular spot, at an upscale Hotel that he used at times like these. Since he had gotten cool with the hotel manager over the years, the manager always let him use the room that was so exclusive that not only was it not listed, but it was also only accessible by having an access card that allowed the elevator to go to the top floor. Devion liked the room because if the female he was with had robbery on her mind, it was impossible for him to get caught slipping.

Entering the room, Honey was amazed by the size of the room that looked more like a luxurious one-bedroom condo. Her eyes took in the 60-inch flat screen television that hung on the wall, a brown buttery leather sectional and an enormous kitchen area. The bedroom was even more impressive with an enormous round bed in the center. The back wall housed a fish tank recessed in the wall filled with all sorts of tropical fish.

Gazing around at the whole room, Honey was impressed. A place like this was something new to her.

Devion broke her train of thought as he spoke. "Look Honey, I appreciate the offer you made, but to tell you the truth I ain't in the pimpin' game, shawty. I ain't got time for all the bullshit and stress that come along with it, feel me?"

She just looked at him and said nothing at first.

He continued, "Don't get it twisted, shawty, I got a pimp's mentality thanks to my father, but if you looking for pimpin', you should holla at my pops, baby girl. I ain't looking fa shit. I get my money how I get my money and just want the females I deal with to be real with me. You say you wanna make me rich? Then show me betta than you can tell me and we'll go from there. Keep breaking bread with a G, stay down, and never lie, and your back will be covered. I'll make sho' you want for nothing, baby girl. You think that's something you could do, lil mamma?" Devion asked.

Honey looked into his eyes and replied, "You told me to show you better than I could tell you, right daddy?"

Once she referred to him as daddy, he knew that she had signed her soul to him and all he said was, "Fo' sho. Look, there's a clean robe hanging on the bathroom door, so go jump that ass in the shower and wipe all those tricks off you. Bring the baby oil when you get through and I'll oil your body if you want me to."

She grinned while making her way toward the bathroom.

Devion grabbed the remote off the coffee table and turned on the TV. The first channel displayed a fireplace with a crackling fire while an R. Kelly R&B song played through the surround sound. Going to the refrigerator, he grabbed one of the many Coronas, then took a seat at the kitchen table and started to break down some of the Kush weed he had to roll in the blunt. With the same remote control, he turned off the main lights and illuminated the many soft lights recessed in the ceiling all throughout the rooms.

Checking his phone to make sure he had no missed calls or messages, he made sure the ringer was on high before he placed it on the charger.

*Damn, I hope everything is what it is and everything goes as planned*, he thought. *I wouldn't mind having a crib like dat nigga Duran's somewhere off in another country and shit.*

Devion was in deep thought and feeling the effects from the blunt when Honey came out of the room, butt ass naked with a small bottle of baby oil in her hand. She stood in the doorway with one hand on her hip staring at Devion before she asked, "Do you want me to come out or are you going to oil me up in the bedroom?"

Devion looked at her body in amazement! *Damn! I done seen some bad bitches in my life, but dis here is a straight beauty* he thought to himself. Aloud he said, "Come over here by the couch, ma," while he rose and walked over to the sofa as well.

Before he put the blunt out in the ashtray, he extended it to her to see if she smoked. She took it and gave him the body oil. Grabbing a fur blanket from under the coffee table, he spread it over the couch so the couch wouldn't get oily from her body.

Since he was taught to always think with the head with the brain instead of the one with the vein, he had no problem oiling her body from head to toe while just having a conversation and enjoying the beauty that laid before him.

Because of the way he behaved, she liked him even more. Most men wouldn't have even been able to finish the simple act of putting oil on her before they would be trying to get some ass.

When Devion finished, he got up and grabbed another beer from the fridge and also poured himself a glass of Remy. He came back to the couch and opened a box that was on the table. With the scoop inside, he dumped a little powder on the table.

"You get down?" Devion asked Honey.

"Naw, daddy I use to, but left it alone about two years ago," she said while turning to lie on her side.

"Dat's what's up and whether you know it or not, that's a plus in my book," Devion commented.

While getting high off the coke, Devion saw Honey rubbing on her thigh from the corner of his eye. With each stroke, she kept going higher and higher until she brushed past her neatly trimmed pubic hairs. Then with her fingers, she grazed the outer walls of her vagina.

Devion sipped his drink and did another line as if he hadn't noticed what Honey was doing.

But she knew he was watching and she kept going. With her fingertips, she massaged her clit and closed her eyes. Then, she dipped her finger into the tight, warm, and wet inner walls of her pussy.

Letting out a gentle moan, she kept stroking herself until they both heard the gushing sound her pussy made as it got wetter and wetter.

Now, Devion no longer pretended not to notice. Being turned on by Honey's show, he lit a cigarette, sat back and continued to watch.

She opened one eye slightly and got turned on even more at the sight of Devion sitting back cool, calm and collected just watching her do her thang.

Honey moaned louder and she gyrated her hips to her own pleasure rhythm until she came and squirted all over the blanket, leaving a puddle. After a few seconds, she rose up and stood. Then slowly and seductively, she walked over to Devion licking her juices clean off her fingertips.

"Sweet or sour?" Devion asked

"Why don't you find out, Daddy," Honey shot back at him.

Devion stood, grabbed Honey by her waist, lifted her up, then sat her in the same spot where he'd been sitting.

"Oooh, shit, this couch is so cold," Honey said.

"That's what the robe was for," Devion shot back at her. They both laughed.

Squatting down on his knees, Devion placed Honey's legs over his shoulders and he kissed the inner parts of her thighs. He planted soft sensual kisses until he placed a gentle kiss on her pearl tongue.

Devion knew he had skills with turning women out with his head game and he had Honey damn near biting her lip off as she moaned and enjoyed pure ecstasy. He placed a finger in her vagina, then a finger in her ass.

It was a feeling she had never experienced before and in just a few minutes, he had her skeeting all over his mustache.

"Oooh. Daddy," she panted. "Why you do me like dat?"

"You did tell me to find out whether it was sweet or sour, did you not?" Wiping his face with his forearm, "And sweet it is. I may need to check for a cavity" he said with a grin. Then he sat back on the couch next to her before he took another sip of his drink. He fired up the half of a blunt that had gone out as Honey's breathing finally returned to normal and she gained her composure.

She reached over and pulled his shirt over his head, admiring his toned, tattooed arms before she unhooked his belt buckle.

While sliding his pants off, Devion took his pistol that had been tucked in his waistband and placed it on the table. But Honey didn't seem to notice the gun. Her eyes were on the bulge in his boxers before she got down in between his legs and slid his boxers off.

What she found, she didn't expect to see. Of course, she knew that he was probably a good size from his swagger, but she didn't imagine that he would be that thick.

"Damn Papi! Yo dick do push ups, too?" she said.

Devion just gave her a grin before she put her warm, wet, welcoming mouth on his penis. She got it wet and slippery at first. Then she licked him from the base of his dick to the head as if it were a candy cane. She sucked on his balls while stroking his Johnson at the same time. She took all of him into her mouth again and started to go deeper as her jaws loosened and he became more lubricated.

Honey took pride in her head and the ability she had to deep throat, but she was beginning to think that she wasn't going to be able to fit him all in her mouth. But since he was going to be her new man, she went for the gusto and swallowed his entire dick until the tip hit the back of her throat. She started to gag, but she didn't stop until that reflex disappeared, and a tear formed in her eyes.

Devion looked down at her as she looked back at him and was immediately turned on by the tears welling in her eyes.

Then, he stood up and she rocked back as she leaned back and welcomed the cum Devion showered onto her face.

With her finger, she scraped some of it off her cheek and placed it in her mouth. She grinned at him as she stood, then sauntered toward the bathroom. When she came out, Devion was standing in the bedroom by the bed wearing nothing but ankle socks. He had already placed his gun under a pillow on the floor next to his bed because he never slept without his gun being close by.

She approached him and pushed him toward the bed until he fell onto the mattress. Then, she straddled him, putting his already protected dick deep within her walls. While she rode him with slow strokes up and down around and around, he sucked on her breasts and nibbled on her nipples. He cuffed her ass and guided her with each stroke, pulling her ass cheeks apart while he thrust every inch of his manhood deeper and deeper inside of her. They moved together, almost simultaneously going faster and faster. He kept going until he started to hear her pussy fart.

"Yes baby, right there! You're hitting my spot, daddy," Honey screamed while she reached back and grabbed his balls.

Devion rolled over and placed Honey on her stomach. He gave her deep, long, slow strokes. "Grab your ass and pull your cheeks apart," he commanded.

She did as she was told and minutes later, they both had multiple orgasms before they laid down, completely worn out.

"Damn, lil momma, you got some good pussy," Devion said, stroking Honey's ego.

"And you got a big ass dick," she replied returning the favor.

He was quiet for a moment before he told her, "Look Honey, these next couple of weeks gon' be a lil hectic for me, but I want you to check in wit me daily to let me know you straight. In the meantime in between time, I want you to be strictly 'bout business and getting on top of your shit. For me, it's business first and ass last. Ya feel me?"

"I know you 'bout your paper, daddy, and I wanna do whatever it takes to make sure you stay on top and beyond. But like you said, I gotta show you betta than I can tell you, so you know what? Handle your business, baby, but make sure you be careful so you can get back to me. And when you come back, I'ma show you just how real I am, okay?"

"Alright, I got you, but look if you too tired to drive home right now, I can get you another room till you rest up."

"Naw, I'm good, but what, You have to leave now?" She paused and glanced over at the clock. "It's only 5:45, baby."

"Yea, I need to meet up with my brother," was all Devion said. "I'm about to jump in the shower so I can get ready to roll, you joining me?"

Without hesitation, Honey jumped up and ran into the bathroom first. She had started the shower water before he'd even gotten out of the bed. She opened the glass shower door, stepped in and relished in the feel of the warm water hitting her body. She anxiously awaited her new man's arrival to join her for some early morning lovemaking under the cascading waters before they departed. □

# Chapter 9

Walking into his apartment at a quarter til 7, Devion saw his brother in the living room in a pair of gym shorts, a muscle tee, and some Jordan flip flops. He was sitting on the couch, smoking a blunt and drinking orange juice. But it was his facial expression that said that he was in some type of deep thought.

"What's happening, bro?" Devion said, throwing his keys on the table.

"Shit, what's good with you, D? Was everything straight last night?"

"I'm good; yea, everything was straight. Just kicked it with shawty, got knee deep in some good ass pussy," Devion joked. He laughed and gave his brother a fist bump.

"Already!" Kevion said.

Devion nodded and then asked his brother. "Wuzzup with you, tho? You sent shawty home already?"

"Naw, she in the bed sleep right now. We just chilled last night, tho, my mind was too far gone thinking about this lick and how much money we gon' make if everything goes the way it's supposed to go. Feel me?"

"Dats wuzzup. Funny thang 'bout that is, the whole time I was tryna break shawty's back, my mind was on the same thing. I know we makin' some nice change out here in these streets, but I hope this shit is what it is too, bro. You see Duran's and Mom's and Pop's crib? I'm trying to get my pockets like that, ya dig?" Devion said.

"I know Pops would break us off whatever we want, but I'm my own man and can you imagine how powerful we'll be if we all had cake up to the sky?"

"Yea, I can imagine," Kevion said.

"So what time we gon' hit Duran up, KD?"

"I was thinking about ten or eleven. You know not to be too early, but to let him know we about our paper, ya dig?"

"Like a shovel, bro. I'm 'bout to whip up some pancakes, eggs, and sausage, you want some?"

"Yea, hook it up; I'm 'bout to get shawty up so she can go handle her business. Do me a favor and make a lil extra in case she's hungry."

"I got you bro."

It was around 10:30, after they'd had breakfast and Hershey was gone, that Kevion dialed Duran's number. He, put the phone on speaker, then placed it on the table so both he and Devion could hear.

After just a couple of rings, Duran answered, "Que paso, amigos?"

"Hey, how you doing, Mr. Duran?" They said in unison, something the Twins always seemed to do.

"I'm good, my boys. I hope you took care of everything you needed to do, because as soon as you go talk to your father this weekend, everything's a go. Those two lovely ladies you met who brought you here, Cleopatra and Zolandria, are going to be bringing you the first of many shipments and also letting you know who you need to contact to get you two jump started."

"Alright, dats wuzzup. So what do we need to do in the meantime, Mr. Duran?" Devion said speaking up.

"Just continue to lay low, but also inform the major players in the game, the ones that you trust, that the best product for a cheaper price is coming to town. But other than that, just chill out and go spend some time with your mother. I hear she's expecting, so hang out with her from time to time, comprende?"

"Do we call you again or what?" Kevion asked.

"No, Cleo has your numbers and she will call you to set up the meeting, alright? I have some business to take care of but I'll be in touch. I'll talk to you two later."

"A'ight, Mr. D, we'll holla, stay up, G," Devion said.

"You two do the same," Mr. Duran said before hanging up.

After hanging up, the Love Boys sat back in their chairs while a smile formed on both of their faces.

**********************

As she eagerly waited for him in the bathtub with fifty candles lit all around the bathroom, she submerged herself in the water and soaked in the very warm bubble bath laced with the baby oil that he had prepared for her.

He finally walked in, puffing on a Kush filled cigar and handed her a glass of wine. She took a few sips and felt all tingly inside. Then, she took a puff on his cigar, before she placed it in the ashtray. Grabbing the washcloth, she lathered it. He lowered the cover on the toilet and sat down.

"Give me your foot," he said, patting his knee. Starting at the sole of her foot, he gently massaged, causing her to burst into a girlish squeal. She tried to pull her foot away, but he held her tight.

"Stop, that tickles," she screamed.

But he didn't stop. He tickled her once more for good measure, before letting her foot go.

He laughed and grabbed the washcloth. He caressed her leg as he washed her, allowing the washcloth and his hand disappear beneath the water before rubbing the inner part of her thigh.

She was eager for him to go further, to clean the more delicate parts of her body, but she waited patiently and kept her inner thoughts contained. She had confidence in her man, knowing that he was going to do his job.

Right when the thought passed through her mind, she felt one of his fingers gently brush against her asshole and then his fingers glided upwards and forwards towards her pinocha.

He stroked her pearl tongue, simply wanting to create a pulsating beat while teasing her at the same time.

Then, he returned to washing her and after finishing up the rest of her legs, arms, and of course, her tempting full figured breasts, he said, "Now turn over and get on all fours and make sure you got that dip in your back while you bust that ass open."

Without hesitation, she was on all fours with her big ass booty tooted up in the air.

While looking back and observing him attempting to maintain his composure, she became a comedian. "You like this, Daddy?" she asked.

Her words made him pop her on the ass which sent tremors and shakes from her ass all the way through her spine. She liked that and wiggled her ass at him. Without a word, she was asking for him to give her more because it hurt so good!

After lathering up the washcloth once more, he scrubbed her back, starting from her shoulders, all the way down her spine. After washing the back of her thighs, he delicately began to clean and rub her flower. He knew that it was turning her on from the way she shifted her body.

Finally, he raised the washcloth from the water, and then ran it under the faucet to warm it up again. Then, he squeezed it, letting the water rinse her body.

The heat of the water relaxed her. "Ooh baby, that feels good," she moaned with her eyes closed.

He pushed himself off the toilet and got on his knees. Then, he pushed a breath of air through his lips.

The light gust of wind sent chills up past her asshole all the way up to her clitoris. And before she could even turn around to see what was going on, his wet, warm, tongue has already licked her pearl tongue and the inside of her pussy walls. He went deep inside of her, fucking the shit out of her with his tongue. He gently stroked and rubbed her asshole, giving her double pleasure. She started to move in a circular motion and quickly matched the rhythm and rotation of his tongue and lips. He slurped, and licked, and blew deep into her.

With one hand, she grasped the edge of the tub to balance herself. And with her other hand, she reached behind and held his head, guiding him.

While feasting on her pussy just right, he felt her tense up as she began to moan and cuss uncontrollably. Then her body shot into convulsions.

Knowing that she'd had multiple orgasms, he wiped his mouth and face with a towel hanging from the bar on the wall while leaving her in another world still, on all fours.

He grabbed his glass that he'd rested on the sink and took a swig of his Remy Martin, and fired his blunt back up.

It still took her a moment to break out of her trance and regain her composure. She turned and looked at him as he was sitting back down on the toilet, smoking his blunt.

When she stood, he took her whole body in with his lust filled eyes. As he watched her, she rubbed her breasts and squeezed them together before her hand slowly descended down, past her stomach before she stopped and dipped her fingers into her love box. She gently glided and stroked her pussy, putting on a show for him until her fingers were nice and wet from busting another nut. Then, she licked her fingers clean and once she was done with that, she dropped to her knees and unbuckled his belt, before unbuttoning his pants.

While staring eye to eye with a handful of meat between her oiled fingers, she slowly stroked his semi hard dick until it rocked up like that old Chevy commercial, "Like a rock". While caressing his nuts, she wondered if she could take him all in. So she went for it and was almost successful, but then, she gagged and damn near threw up. She was forced to retreat and back away.

She dusted herself off from the embarrassment and decided to try it again. She regained her composure and started to build back the momentum by starting off sucking lightly on his nuts. While remaining cool, calm, and collected like a Big Dog is supposed to, he took another swig of the potent drink.

She pulled his pants and boxers to the floor so that he could easily step out of them. He stood up, which forced her to sit on her heels and lean her head back so that she could even lick the backside of his nut sack like she wanted and how he wanted her to do.

"Damn baby girl, you'za freaky bitch, ma," was all he could say while placing a hand on the wall for balance. He had to hold on to keep from falling because her skills and desire to please him was causing his knees to get weak. "Shit!"

After creating a lot of saliva and storing it up in her mouth, she knew that her nigga was reaching his climax by the pre-nut that was starting to seep out onto her hand as she stroked him. She took one more lick and blew on his balls to return the favor from him blowing in the crack of her ass. Then, she started sucking on his head.

Knowing that pleasing her man was as much of a turn on for her as for him, he maintained discipline by not grabbing the beautiful filthy bitch by her head to fuck on her tonsils. Instead, he grabbed his blunt, lit it back up, making her stop long enough to take a charge. He smoked his blunt while letting her finish the job she set out to do.

This time, she warmed herself up and took more and more of him in until her eyes squeezed tight. Her eyes teared while she deep throated him. Feeling his nuts expand in her hand, she sucked, sucked, and sucked with a whole lot of spit, spit, spit until he pulled her by her hair making her lean back, and then he showered her with all the built up cum all over her hair, face, and body.

After it had stopped raining, she took him back into her mouth to drain and lick up every last drop of the protein and to keep his manhood still on hard. After quickly jumping in the tub to wipe her face and body, he lifted her out of the tub and laid her back onto the rug on the bathroom floor. Looking into her eyes, he stuck his hand inside of her, while moving it in and out, rubbing her clit to tease her. He then placed his arm underneath hers and grabbed a fistful of her hair.

Pulling her head back to expose her neck, he went in like he was Dracula on the hunt for blood. Biting and sucking on her neck while going deeper and deeper inside of her with his manhood, each time coming all the way out just to plunge back in.

He began to lick and play with that soft spot just below and behind her ear. She moaned while she scratched his ass with her nails. He blew into her ear just before sticking his tongue deep inside. Eventually, he made his way to the part of her body that he had under complete control. He twirled and hit every corner, dip, and wall inside of her warm, wet, tight pussy, as she screamed, moaned, groaned and nutted while he growled, howled, licked and kissed her.

Then, all of a sudden, he heard, "Robinson! Get up and get ready! You have a visit in forty-five minutes," the guard shouted.

It took him a moment to fully wake up and break out of his dream. He could've sworn it was real.

"Damn!" he said out loud. Getting out of bed and grabbing his toiletry bag he thought to himself, *Back to this shit. Nigga gotta jump in the shower. Boxers are feeling sticky. The dream was fire though! Nigga might have to get another special visit in a few, especially with some of that pregnant pussy. Let me get my ass up and go see the family.*

# Chapter 10

"Hey baby, how you doing my love?" Brandie greeted her kid's father as he approached the table.

"I'm living, my queen, maintaining and staying a couple more steps ahead of the game," Derry Don said back at her. Then, he turned to his sons. "Wuzzup, boys? Y'all ain't got no holla for ya old man?"

"Naw it ain't nothing like that. What's up, Pops?" Devion said giving his dad some dap and a hug.

"How you doing, Pops, you straight? Kevion asked.

"I'm good, even better now seeing the three of y'all. I know you two probably have a lot of questions about what has transpired these last couple of weeks, but right now, I need you to understand that I did what I thought was best for you two. We'll have a lot of time for questions later, but for now I need to lay down the game plan that'll keep you safe but at the same time make you a lot of money."

Brandie knew that this visit was about business, so she sat patiently allowing her men to talk. Besides, she knew the next visit would be a one-on-one with the man she loved and if he could pull some strings to get them a much needed special visit.

"Now boys, you have already re-met Zolandria and Cleopatra and you've taken a trip to meet Duran. He's a long time friend and I do trust him with my life, so I shouldn't have to ask you to give him the same respect as you would give me. With that being said, by the time y'all make it home, the girls will be calling you to get directions to where they should unload the product. I know you deal mainly with coke and that shouldn't be a problem with you getting rid of, but they are going to tie y'all in with some heavy players that move heroin. You two already have a solid team built, so I advise y'all to take them out of the trap houses and make them your top dogs. For now on Noah, TK, JoJo, and C-Biscuit do only what you do and that's watching each other's back. Making only the big sales and making sure the other employees keep shit straight and count money."

"What other employees, dad?" Kevion asked.

"The ones you're going to have to hire. Just because I said I want you two out of the trap doesn't mean you should shut it down. To my understanding, you've already made them look abandoned, so when you put new faces in there, all the heat from the streets would be directed in another direction. I'm not going to tell you how much to pay them but pay them well. Remember, as long as the team eats, you eat. I have an old warehouse already set up in South Dallas where you'll make all the big business transactions. Cleo has the keys and she'll show you where it's at."

It felt like they had just gotten there when the guard came over to them. "Robinson, five minutes, wrap it up."

"Alright, boys, I know you two are about your business, so I don't have to waste time telling you nothing you already know. Make sure you watch each other's backs and always be on guard. And remember, slippa's count, too." Then, he turned to

Brandie. "Baby girl, you make sure you're here next weekend, ma. Take care of my unborn seed, lil girl."

Raising to his feet, he dapped his sons up and embraced his queen in a long hug and kiss.

"I'll see you later, love," Dante' said softly.

The twins walked to the parking lot with their mother. Brandie was crying as she always did after visiting Dante'. She hated leaving him behind the barbed wire that had become a painful reminder of the one costly mistake that had haunted them and created a domino effect of changes in their lives. Nevertheless, her love and respect for him would never allow her to voice that disappointment.

Since they arrived at the facility in separate cars, the twins kissed their mother and watched her drive away before getting back into their car. The Love Boys were on I-75 heading back to Oak Cliff when Kevion's phone rang.

"Yo, it's Cleo, D," Kevion said to his brother, letting him know who was calling.

"Hey, what's up, lady?" Kevion answered.

"Hey, Kevion, text me the address to the new spot so I can map it out and meet you there, Papi. The shipment came in today."

After he had given her the address, he told Devion to call TK and JoJo to let them know to meet them at 10 that night, while he called Noah and Curtis to tell them the same.

******************************

When they made it to the safe house, both of the women were already there waiting in a U-Haul moving truck.

"Damn, these bitches in a fucking U-Haul, bro," Devion said. "I feel like our game just went up one hundred thousand percent."

They unlocked the house door from inside the garage before unlocking the roll top door to the U-Haul. When they opened it, all they saw were boxes on top of boxes. By the time they offloaded everything from the truck into the house, they had unloaded two hundred boxes.

"Look gentlemen," Cleopatra spoke. "There's one hundred boxes per product. One hundred are filled with Heroin and one hundred with Coke. Each one has five keys bundled in them, so you do the math."

And that's exactly what they did.

*Five times one hundred equals five hundred times two equals one thousand.* For the first time, Devion was speechless. All he could do was smile at the numbers and dollar signs that began to float around in his head.

"And here boys are the keys to the warehouse and here's a prepaid phone with the connections you need to call either tonight or in the morning. They are already waiting for your call because it's about that time for them to re-up. As you know, every key of coke goes for thirty-five grand and the heroin goes for ninety."

"Ninety? Goddam!" Devion said excitedly. "That's what?"

"That's forty-five million, bro," Kevion said doing the math quickly in his head.

"That's right," Cleopatra added. "But like Duran said, this is just a jump starter to get things moving. Listen, your father is counting on you boys; he's still making moves, but with your help on the streets, y'all will be able to make the connections that are just too risky for him to make from behind those walls."

"Alright Cleo, but show us where the warehouse is so we can make it back for our meeting with the crew."

After getting the location and inspecting the warehouse, they made it back in time for the meeting.

During the meeting, the Love Boys promoted their top dogs and explained to them that on that shipment alone, they were bound to make a little over forty-six million dollars. Everyone in the crew was excited and eager to start. They agreed to meet back up at the house at 7:30 the next morning. The brothers jumped in Kevion's car and headed home.

On the way home, Devion's phone rang.

"Hey, what's up? Tell me something good."

"Hey, Daddy, were you busy, baby?" Honey asked.

"No, I'm good right now. What's up?"

"Can I see you tonight?" Honey asked.

"I wish I could, ma, but I have a really busy day tomorrow and I need to get some type of sleep, baby girl."

"Please, it won't take long; I need to give you something. Just tell me where to meet you and I'll be there."

"A'ight look, I'm rollin with my brother so he'll be with me, but meet me at the Mickey D's on Lancaster Road. How long is it going to take you to get there because I'm about five minutes away?"

"It'll take me ten, Daddy. I'm on my way now."

"A'ight, baby girl. I'll be there."

After waiting only four minutes after they arrived, Honey pulled up next to them. Devion got out of the car, and Honey got out of hers and they greeted each other.

"So what was so urgent that couldn't wait, shawty?"

Without another word, Honey went to the trunk of her car, opened it and pulled out a small duffel bag. "Here," she said. She gave Devion a kiss on the cheek and told him to call once he got some free time to spend with her.

Devion liked that she respected his schedule and didn't try to hold him up with small talk. She came, did what she had to do and left. Devion didn't open the bag until he and Kevion got back on the freeway. As soon as he opened the stuffed bag, one hundred dollar bills poured out.

"Damn bro, what you do to that girl?" Kevion asked.

Looking up with a smile on his face, Devion said, "Just being me, bro. She keep this shit up, she's definitely going to earn a permanent spot on the team."

"Yea, shawty trying to make sure she on the team," Kevion added.

In the back of Devion's mind, he was indeed pleased with Honey's actions and wanted to see just how far he could go with her. He sent her a text with just a smiley face on it.

Tired from the long day, they arrived at their house, went to their separate rooms to shower and get some rest.

# Chapter 11

The next morning the team met back at the house and Kevion called the first numbers that were in the phone. The first number was for some cat named Mickey that had an "H" by his name. Kevion figured the "H" stood for heroin and that's exactly what Mickey wanted.

He told Kevion that he needed one hundred of them, talking in code through the whole conversation. Kevion told him where to meet and Mickey told him he would be there at eleven. After calling the rest of the numbers and getting their orders, if everything went right that night, they would have 50 kilos of boy and 150 kilos of coke left.

When they drove to the warehouse to make the first drop, everyone's nerves were on edge, even though they took precaution by traveling in three separate cars, with the product in the middle of the three. They got to the warehouse with no mishaps and arrived early enough to set up shop. All of them were strapped with handguns, and for extra protection, Noah and Curtis each had choppers (automatic assault rifles). Mickey arrived with three other workers who worked for him.

After Kevion and Devion had greeted him, Mickey's workers put three large duffel bags, each filled with three million dollars on the table. After they had inspected the money to make sure there wasn't any trash in it, they gave them two boxes that had 50 keys in each.

By the end of the day, they had made all of the business deals at the warehouse. Luckily they had invested in some money counting machines. Otherwise, it would have taken them all night to count the money. When they finished, they were now forty-six million five hundred thousand dollars richer.

"Hey, TK and JoJo, tomorrow I want y'all two to go to South Dallas and holla at them chicks y'all know that be fucking with that boy. Let them know we on and we gon' have it for cheaper than what they are paying now and it's twice as good," Devion said.

"Take them a sample to let one of them dope heads try it out so they can see what it do with their own eyes," Kevion said.

"Me and Devion gonna go holla at Loc and get shit pop'n. Noah, I need you to get those young cats that be on the block in the hood pushing them petty rocks and put them in the trap houses and hit them off with some packs. Take a key and break it in half to put in the two houses. That's just to start them off with. Let's put this money in the safe and get in grind mode so we can let Duran know we ain't playing out here. It's too much money to be made and I know I'm trying to get it."

Devion rolled up a blunt and poured each one of them up a glass of Hennessey. He took some coke out of the key that was to go to the trap houses and tested it out. "Damn G! My muthufuckin' face is numb."

After they had put the money up, they toasted their glasses and smoked a blunt. Each one of them left knowing that they were now millionaires and eager to earn more.

********************************

Leaving the safe house riding to the sounds of Young Jeezy pouring through the speakers, the boys couldn't believe how their lives had taken a step in a whole new direction in such a short period of time.

"Damn bro, can you believe this shit?" Devion said. "We done made over forty million just that fast."

"Yea, I feel you bro, it's like I'm waiting for someone to wake me up and tell me it's all a dream, know what I'm saying?"

"And you just think, it ain't like we gotta take that money to invest in mo' shit, cuz long as it rains on them fields, we gotta endless supply, so it's all profit."

"Damn, I forgot all about that shit! Duran has those accounts set up overseas for us to stash that bread. Man, this shit is sweet!"

"Yea, bro, but remember every day we got to play the game like our stomachs touching our backs and we can never get too relaxed with these niggas. Remember Pops always taught us that slippa's do count," Kevion said.

"I'm with you on dat bro. I'm already itchin' for a nigga to jump outta line. Trust me once they draw them lines round his body, he won't be jumpin' out them no mo or even jumpin' at all for that matter."

Kevion laughed but knew his brother was dead serious.

"Yo, we forgot to call the connect, bro," Devion said.

"No, I didn't forget, bro, I want to get through this first shipment first to get our money up before I get at dude. Trust me, I'm thinking of everything and everybody, but first we need to take care of the hood and get everybody on the team. Before you know it, all the major niggas gonna be looking for us. Feel me? Especially when they start to feel their pockets getting light," Kevion added.

"I like how you thinking, bro. Come on let's go holla at Loco. I hope he got the grill fired up. I'm hungrier than a muthafucka,"Devion replied.

They pulled up to their friend's house and the moment they walked in the door, Loco said, "The muthufuckin' Love Boys! What's crackin' cuz?"

"What's good, OG? What you got going, Loc?"

"Shit, I'm coolin'; you know hook'n up a lil sum'n- sum'n up. Nigga gotta eat, right?"

"Fa sho," Devion replied giving his friend some dap.

"What y'all niggas got up? Y'all seen ya pops lately?"

"Yea, we just saw him yesterday as a matter of fact. He straight, up in that bitch getting big and shit staying on top of his game."

" Word, that's wuzzup. I miss my nigga on the real."

"You know that shit we were talking 'bout last time I was here?" Kevion asked

"Yea, so what's crackin'?" Loco asked.

"All I gotta say is that your old connect need to get at us now. Nigga, we on and I'm talkin' about in a major way. And for your family, instead of paying that thirty you was paying, you get them for twenty-five and if you getting two or mo', they gon' be twenty. That's just for you bro, dig? Everybody else gonna have to come with that thirty folk."

"Nigga, you stunt'n, bro," Loc said, not believing what he was hearing.

"You got two of them things on you now?" he asked.

"Fuck no. What? You think we just ridin' around with keys in these streets?" Devion said. "I can drop them off early in the morning if you can wait."

"Fa that price! Hell yea, I can wait! I got just enough to last me through the night, but I need them joints first thing in the morning though, lil G's."

"That's a bet. I'll get those to you before we start the day off," Kevion said. "It's going to be about six, straight?"

"Yea, I'll be still up," Loco said.

"Nigga, fix me one of them plates; nigga starvin 'round this bitch."

"Y'all must've been grindin' all day," Loco said. "But yo nigga don't act brand new. You know where the plates are at Negro and your muthufuckin hands ain't broke. As a matter of fact, grab me a couple of them Colt 45's out the fridge, young nigga."

"I got you," Devion said.

Devion never took orders from no one, but for the family he was down for the cause.

By the time Kevion and Devion dropped off the two keys to Loco the next day, and made it back to the safe house, it had started raining with the sky full of clouds. It was around 6:30 when a call came in.

"Hey Kevion, this is Cleo. How are you boys coming along?"

"Hey Cleo, everything is straight on this end" he replied.

"We are almost done with the initial supply and thinking we are gonna need some more by the weekend. What you doing up so early, ma?"

"Early? Well, it's not enough light in the daytime, Papi. Besides, your dad got me like this. My body is trained and used to being up by five. You boys move fast and hustle hard, I see. As soon as you run out, call Duran and he'll arrange another shipment."

"Tell me something, Cleo," Kevion said.

"What is it?"

"I know when we gotta re-up, you two not going to be pulling up in the U-Haul, are you? The folks in the area see a truck come through every other week to the same house, they gonna start getting nosey, mami, ya feel me?"

Laughing, Cleopatra said, "No honey, we are not coming like that anymore. If you noticed when I gave you the keys to the warehouse, it was two sets. Right next to the warehouse is another building you are going to use for storage. Trust me, the amount of shipments coming through won't be able to fit inside the house. You and I are the only ones with keys, so get a copy for your brother and an extra to be put in a safe place. I was just calling to see how business was going and if you needed anything."

"Naw, shawty, we are straight. I'll call you if we do, though."

"Okay, then. I'll let you two get back to your business."

"Alright, Cleo. I'll holla at you later," Kevion said before hanging up.

"Yo, what she want?" Devion asked.

"She just wanted to see how we were doing, but she told me that building next door to the warehouse is the new spot where we gonna keep all the product."

"Word?" Devion said.

"Yea, I was wondering how we were going to handle that. You know we got some nosey ass neighbors and shit, Devion."

About that time, Noah walked into the house.

"Yo, what's up family?" Noah said walking through the door puffing on a blunt.

"What's good, son?" Kevion said.

"Shit, I'm coolin, just came from the spot," Noah replied.

You got it jumpin' already, family?" Devion asked.

"Yea, bro. I ain't been to sleep yet. I was up all night and grabbed up a few niggas off the block soon as I left here last night. I broke Steve and Vince off some of that shit, D-Mac. You shoulda seen them niggas skitz the fuck out. 'Bout time twelve o'clock rolled around, that bitch was pumpin', Jack. I'm 'bout to lay it down for a couple hours befor' I get the other spot jumpin' off. I already gave them three niggas five G's a piece and trust me, they already know how D-Mac get down and they don't want no parts of that."

"Them niggas some wise niggas," Devion said while taking the blunt from Noah.

"Call me 'bout five, tho, to make sho I'm up, family."

"I got you," Kevion said. "Yo, let TK and JoJo in when they get here. We 'bout to go holla at Nick 'n them," Kevion told Noah.

"Yea, a'ight. Tell folk I said what it do for me, ya dig."

"One."

"What up, Lil Gangstas'," Nick greeted the Love Boys as they came through the door of his apartment in North Dallas. Nick was a Gangsta Disciple, so it was always "Gangster this" or "Folk that" when he talked; and since their father had been affiliated with the Gangster Nation, he always called KD and D-Mac Lil Gangsters.

"We chill'n, fool," Kevion said while dappin' him up with a hug.

"Out'chere getting dis' money," Devion added. "What you got poppin'?"

"Shit, folk I'm coolin', I just got back from handling a lil business, you know. Some lil punk ass niggas was caught short stopping one of the spots last night, so I went to go holla at him. I tried to talk with him and let him know I wasn't knocking his hustle, doing my best to let him make it. Nigga must've not known 'bout me cuz the nigga started poppin' off at the mouth, talking about how he was taking ova the block and he was gonna do whatever he felt. By the time he opened his mouth to say something else, he had two in his head already pushin' daisies."

"Damn Unc, you shoulda hit me up on that one," Devion said. "You know how much I like a lil action."

"I would have if I was going ova there for that, but like I said, I tried to let the nigga make it. He made his own bed, so I hope he made the bitch with a lot of cushion, cuz he gon' forever lay in the muthafucka."

Devion and Kevion laughed.

"So what brings you boys through?"

"We came to let you know we're on with the coke game. You know we had to come through and let you know what's up."

Devion added, "whatever price you paying now is way too much for what we gon' give it to you for."

Laughing, Nick said, "I guess your dad finally turned y'all on to D."

"Damn, you know about Duran too?" Kevion asked.

"Lil G's, where you think I get my shit from? You think your old man wasn't gon' turn me on to the plug? Shit, I been fuckin' with them for about ten years now. Me and my partna' G both do. You know G quit fuckin' with that Jamaican cat, so he turned him on too and that's where he get all his shit from now. We been getting our shit from two females that fuck with your pops."

"Who? Cleopatra and Zolandria?" Devion asked.

He nodded. "So I guess he introduced, well re-introduced them to you as well. So I guess since he put y'all down, we gon' be getting everything from y'all now."

"Say Unc, since you haven't killed Duran yet, he must be a pretty loyal dude, huh?" Kevion asked. "I know how protective you are with my dad; he told us how you and Chicago took a liking to him when he was only thirteen and put him down with the Folk Nation," Kevion said.

"Yea, Duran straight. I know when I first met him I didn't trust the cat, but he proved he was a loyal dude way back when, especially when he killed a couple of cats that was talking behind your old man's back not knowing that he was your pops Ace Boon Coon. When he pulled that stunt off, I knew he would ride or die for my nigga."

"Yea, I know, my pops told me to trust him, but I just had to get some reassurance, dig?" Kevion said.

"Datz wuzzup folk," Nick said.

"So you straight, Unc?" Devion said while glancing around the apartment.

"Yea, I'm good right now, I just got five of them thangs from them chicks the other day. My spots do 'bout five a week on a regular and I get rid of 'bout seventy-five a month on the strength of your dad. So every Friday I get my five, and when I hit y'all up, that's for the other business. You feel me?"

Kevion gave Nick a fist bump and replied, "Yea, I got you Unc, but look, on them other deals, bring them cats to the warehouse we got set up in the South. When you know you got one coming, I'ma come scoop you up to show you where we at, a'ight?"

"That's a bet."

Devion told his brother, "Yo, TK just called and let me know he was on the way back to the house to drop the bread off."

Kevion turned to Nick and said, "Alright Unc, we about to smash the gas and be out, much love."

"Y'all lil G's be careful out there," Nick said while dapping both of the boys up.

"And next time you get even a smidgen of trouble, make sho you call me," Devion said.

Laughing, Nick said, "A'ight gangsta, I got you and I'm 'bout to hit G up and let him know what's up."

□

# Chapter 12

"Hey, Mr. Duran, this is Kevion. How you doing?" he asked as he pressed his phone closer to his ear.

"Oh, Kevion I'm doing okay for an old man. How are you and your brother?"

"We maintaining, taking care of business as usual."

"So what's up, you don't have any problems do you?" Duran asked with a hint of concern in his voice.

"Naw, we good, but actually we do have a lil dilemma. You see, some clients of ours are in need of some product, but we don't have enough to fill the order."

"Hold up, wait a minute. You mean to tell me that you two have almost run out already? It hasn't even been a week. I know I provided you two with some contacts to help you get started, but I still thought it would take you at least a week and a half or two," Duran said excitedly.

This took Duran by surprise and he couldn't help but think to himself, *Damn, if these boys keep hustling like that, they gon' make some serious cash flow.*

"Yea, we need to re-up our supply. We appreciate the connections you provided, but you gotta understand, me and my brother both have stomachs that are touching our backs with a never ending pit," Kevion said.

Duran understood what he meant by that terminology and he chuckled before saying, "Okay, tell you what. I'm going to send twice the amount and it'll be there in two days, is that okay?"

"Yes sir, that's straight, they can wait a couple of days. Trust me ain't nobody in the streets got what we got. I'm on my way to deposit the money to the account you had set up for us, alright?" Kevion said.

"So tell me who's in your crew?" Duran asked.

"Besides my brother, our top dawgs are my big cousins TK and JoJo and our brother from another mother, Noah. We also got six cats from the hood working in the spots, and they move about three a piece each week," Kevion told Duran.

"Alright, tell you what. You and your top dawgs each keep a million and pay your workers twenty grand a month. That'll keep them hungry and loyal to you. Remember: take care of the ones that take care of you. That's imperative, Kevion," Duran said in a fatherly tone.

"Alright Mr. Duran, I got you. But tell me something, what would I have to do to open some legit businesses? I figure they could be our means for washing the money and at the same time we can also employ some of our family who don't fuck with the game like that."

"I like how you are thinking, Kevion. Tell me, what business adventures are you thinking about, if you don't mind?"

" Well me and Devion were thinking about an upscale strip club, but I was also thinking of a couple of other things: an auto and detail shop, a beauty salon and barber shop, maybe even a cleaners, just to name a few."

"Those are all some good investments, but I gotta tell you, a strip joint is a risky one, but if you do it right, you could not only be successful, but you could also make a lot of money and meet new clientele if you know what I mean."

"I got you, but that's why I said 'upscale.' I don't want no ghetto ass hood shit; I wanna attract businessmen who come after a long day of work from Corporate America."

"Alright, first you have to get a business license and since your club is going to serve alcohol, I'm guessing you would need to get a liquor license as well. I'll tell you what -- give me about a week to talk to the people I need to talk to about getting you all set up and get everything squared away for you and your brother. In the meantime, location is everything, so when you're not busy find the spots where you wanna set up everything and get a price, okay son?" Duran said.

"Already done," Kevion said." And all five of the buildings are $250,000 altogether."

Duran nodded like he was impressed. "I see you two are about your business, your dad taught you well," Duran said. "Okay, well let me get to the business side of things and I'll let you know soon as I know something. Okay?"

"Alright, well when should we be expecting Cleo to call or do we call you in two days?"

"Cleo will call you to meet, okay?"

"Alright. Take care, Mr. Duran."

"You and your brother do the same and how many times do I have to tell you to just call me "D" or if it's better and more comfortable for you, call me Uncle D, okay?"

"Well you already know my dad instilled respect in us, but Uncle D, I can do," Kevion replied.

Duran chuckled and said, "Yea I know your dad."

"Alright, Uncle D, I'll get with you in a bit," Kevion said before hanging up.

"So what Duran talking about?" Devion asked.

"He said we'll be getting another shipment in two days," Kevion told his brother with a huge grin displaying his satisfaction.

Devion clapped his hands and said, "That's wuzzup up! What he say 'bout us opening the strip joint and shit?"

"He liked the ideas and he said to give him a few weeks to get everything situated," Kevion replied.

"Bet. Well check, since we waiting on the dope, I'ma go scoop Honey from work and chill with shawty for a day. I could use some of that good ass pussy to relieve some of this stress, plus she been buggin' 'bout seeing a nigga. But she already knows what time it is. I'll be back tomorrow evening bro. You straight?

Kevion hesitated a little and said, "Yea I'm good bro. Do your thang, but make sure you at the spot by nine tomorrow night. I plan on giving out the rings we bought for the crew. Do me a favor and pick up a few bottles of Moet and some Kush. I also want the workers there to see what we about and what they one day could have, long as they stay down and loyal to the crew. You feel me?"

"I got you, bro, I'm going to make sho everybody's there," Devion replied.

After taking a shower and jumping fresh in a Kenneth Cole suit with some square toes, Devion was out the door to go scoop up his Honey dip from the club. With him, he had a variety of lingerie he copped for Honey and a diamond-crusted ring and bracelet he got when he and his brother decided to purchase rings for the loyal and reliable crew members who had been with them from the start. With the influx of cash they had come into, spending a little less than $100 grand on jewelry was nothing.

*******************************

After spending the night and the majority of the next day with Honey, Devion arrived at the safe house a little after 9:00 to see everyone was there, waiting for him. TK, JoJo, Noah and some dudes they had recruited to help with the growing business, were sitting around playing "Call of Duty" when they noticed Devion walking through the door.

"Hey, what's up, bro?" Noah said greeting Devion.

"What it do, bro," Devion shot back while going to the kitchen to put the champagne he brought in with him on ice before breaking down a cigar of his own, splitting it with his thumbnail and filling it with some Kush.

"Where my bro at?" Devion asked no one in particular.

"He in the back room," JoJo told him.

After hearing Devion come in, Kevion came out of the back room carrying three large duffle bags. He placed a bag by each of the three chairs surrounding the oversized glass formal table which boasted an expensive crystal chess set as its centerpiece. He walked back to the room to retrieve six other smaller bags and placed them on the floor by the wall behind the table.

"Alright all my top dawgs, y'all sit at the table. Up and coming G's, y'all stand around it."

When they all got into place, Kevion continued,

"Look, y'all youngsters look around the table -- these are my top dawgs, my ride or die niggas. These niggas are some of the most loyal niggas y'all will meet. As long as you got their backs and prove yourself to be loyal and some hard working muthafuckas, they'll not only ride behind y'all, they'll lay down they life on the line for y'all." Kevion paused and glared at everyone intensely.

Devion added, "These are my family, and I know y'all cats out the hood getting your grind on and being some real street niggas, and you already know how I gets down. If anyone of y'all have a problem with anything, don't hesitate to call anyone of us. But understand this, betrayal and disloyalty will NOT be tolerated within this family. You with me and my bro now, so we also consider y'all family. Feel me?"

Each one of the youngsters nodded and were standing upright with their hands behind their backs as if they were in the military.

"Alright, I called y'all here because like my brother said, you are now considered family. But I also wanted y'all to see what could be in your future as long as you prove loyal and trustworthy." Kevion placed a ring box before Noah, TK, and JoJo before he gave his brother one and held one in his hand.

"Open it up G's."

They all opened the boxes and found the thick platinum rings with princess cut diamonds encrusted around the band.

"All the rings match," Kevion said. "And those bags by your chairs are yours, too."

Noah grabbed his first, opened it, and saw the large amount of cash that brought a smile on his face.

"I'm hoping I add six more chairs to this table in due time," Kevion said, referring to the workers who were standing.

"No doubt," one of them said sounding like he was eager and excited at the thought of being considered a top dawg.

"Alright, this is for y'all; I want y'all to know that I acknowledge the hard work, but I do know we ain't close to where we wanna be. There's a lot more money to be made out here," Kevion said while handing each of the newcomers a bag of money.

"Hey, one of y'all lil niggas, go get the Moet out the fridge and bring us some glasses," Devion ordered.

"Tonight we are going to toast to our expansion and just chill. Tomorrow it's back to work," Kevion said.

Drinking and smoking through the night, they stayed at the spot, playing Madden on the PS4 while the Love Boys played a few games of chess before they all went to sleep. Knowing that not only was it going to be a busy day but a busy week ahead.

*******************************

After going to their own homes to shower and change clothes, the new recruits went to the houses where they were assigned to straighten up and get ready for the dope supply. They would need to cook and cut the product as they had been instructed. Kevion and Devion's phones had been ringing since earlier that morning; customers were waiting for them to open up shop.

Mickey, their new heroin customer, had also called letting them know that he needed another large amount that day. By twelve, Cleopatra had called Kevion's phone and told him to meet her and Zolandria at the warehouse at one o'clock.

After meeting them at the warehouse, the brothers stored and locked up the 1000 keys of cocaine and 1000 bricks of heroin. Noah grabbed two keys to put one in each spot, doubling up on what he'd done last time.

Kevion called Mickey first since he was the one spending the most money. Mickey arrived 30 minutes later to get 100 bricks of heroin and 50 kilos of coke. Kevion arranged and set up times for the rest of the customers to come and pick up their product.

# Chapter 13

It was going well, as the days and weeks passed. Two months later, the Love Boys were on their seventh shipment and had taken steps to expand into the other businesses that they'd wanted.

They had located property for a detail shop and barber shop and were looking for the optimal location for a beauty shop. Just like they envisioned, most of their employees would be family members of theirs and their workers.

Their booming success did not escape scrutiny and new found haters. A hustler who was known for moving major weight named Big Boy, and wasn't part of the Love Boys group, noticed that his pockets were getting light. He caught wind of who was responsible for his financial status change from a smoker who was running his mouth.

Jealousy, hatred, and envy filled his heart. But most importantly, he wanted his cash to get back to climbing. After finding out who the Love Boys and the crew were, he hired a hit man to take care of the problem for him.

The hit man's name was Rastah, a tall, dark-skinned Jamaican man who had real Rastafarian dreadlocks that hung down past his shoulders.

After speaking with people in the hood, he found out that Devion was a cold blooded killer and Kevion was the businessman of the duo. So he made plans to go after Devion first. For days, he trailed Devion to get a good feel of his schedule and finally after watching him for seven days, he followed him to a Waffle House.

Devion was supposed to be meeting Honey, but when he parked, he didn't see her car. So he got out of his car and headed to the trunk to grab a Corona that he had in an ice chest.

Before he closed the trunk, the Jamaican snuck up behind him. Devion felt the cold steel of the gun on the back of his neck.

*Damn, slippers count* was all that was going through his mind.

In a deep Jamaican accent, Rastah said, "Don't worry, your brother will be joining you soon."

Since Devion didn't fear death, he just laughed even though he knew he was about to be gone.

Then…Boom!

Just like that, the Jamaican fell to the ground. Devion turned around, looked down and saw the blood gushing from his head. Then, he looked up and there was Honey, holding a smoking baby 380.

Crying she said, "Baby I saw him sneaking up on you when I came out the bathroom and I, and I…"

"Shhhh, don't worry about it," Devion said. "Where you park at?"

"On the other side of the building," she said.

"Hurry up and jump in the whip and follow me, baby. Com' on, we ain't got time to waste. Them laws will be here in a minute."

They both jumped into their cars and sped down the highway. Devion drove fast, but he made sure that she stayed right behind him. Honey kept up like an experienced race car driver.

Even though he was exceeding the speed limit, he made a call.

"What's up, bro, everything straight?" Kevion asked when he answered.

"Some nigga just tried to push my shit back, bro. Call up everybody and y'all meet me at the spot!" Devion yelled into the phone. "I'm going to lace you up when I see you."

"Alright, One," Kevion said before he hung up his phone.

Then, talking aloud to himself, he said, "These niggas done fucked up. I'm killing niggas whole families when I find out who behind this shit."

Arriving at the safe house, Devion and Honey parked their cars in the rear entry garage, in case the cameras got their license plates and the cops were looking for them.

"You straight, baby girl?" Devion asked once they made it inside the house.

"Hell naw! I ain't okay. I just killed someone, Devion," Honey said through tears that were falling from her eyes.

"I got that gun for protection, but I always prayed that I wouldn't have to use it. When I came out the bathroom first, I just saw you. But then when I seen that muthafucka creepin' up behind you with a gun in his hand. Baby all I could think about was losing you, and I can't have that. I mean, who was he? Did you know him?" Honey asked.

"Naw, baby girl, I ain't never seen him before, but damn baby, I'm glad you did have a gun on you and damn sho glad you busted his ass before he put a nigga in the dirt."

He handed her some weed and paper.

"Yo' roll this blunt for me, I need to calm my nerves," Devion said while taking a bottle of Remy to the head.

TK and JoJo got to the house first and at the sight of Honey's fine ass dressed in a sleek silk dress with stiletto heels, their first thought was to say something to her. But the killer look in Devion's eyes told them that something was wrong, which might have explained why Kevion called and told them to the spot quickly.

"Yo, you good family?" JoJo asked Devion.

"Naw cuz, I ain't good right now, but I will be in a few," Devion answered.

Inside, he thought, *Yea I'm going to be straight once I make whoever behind this shit bleed.*

When Noah walked in, he saw TK, JoJo, and Devion sitting at the table, but once he saw Honey sitting on the couch alone, he couldn't help himself.

"Yo! Who bitch is that?" Noah asked.

"Watch ya mouth, bro!" Devion said. "If anyone calls her a bitch, it'll be me. That's Honey, family. That's my lil momma," he told them.

"Aww, my bad, family. You know I don't mean no disrespect."

"Yea I know, bro," Devion said.

""So what's the emergency that got us all ova here?" Noah asked.

"I'ma lace all yo' shoes up once everybody here," Devion said.

"Hey, where C-Biscuit at?" Devion asked no one in particular.

"The last time I checked, he was with your brother, so he probably still with him," JoJo answered quickly, sensing the urgency in Devion's voice.

Five minutes later, Kevion and Curtis walked in and since he had heard of the attempted assassination, Curtis didn't pay Honey any mind. He was there to make sure his friends son was safe and find out who had lost their mind and tried to harm him. Kevion spoke to Honey, since he already knew who she was, but he wondered *why the hell Devion would bring her to the house.*

"So what's tha biz, bro?" Kevion asked.

"A'ight, check it. You already know I was going to meet Honey, right? But dig, I gets there and I didn't notice that she had parked on the other side of the building, feel me? So waiting on her, I jumped out my shit to get a brewski out the cooler and before I could close the trunk, all I could feel was cold steel on the back of my neck. Dis bitch ass nigga was a Jamaican, family, cuz he said something and I could hear it all in his accent. But the nigga fucked me up when he said, 'Your brother will be next.' But that ain't all, as you can see right? So I'm laughing at his bitch ass cuz I'll neva give a nigga the satisfaction to even think that I was afraid. But when the shot went off, I knew I was dead. Then I realized that I didn't feel shit. I turned around and baby girl had smoked his bitch ass. While she ran to her car, I went in his pocket and found this phone."

Devion pulled a phone from his pocket and placed it on the table.

"You know who dis nigga was?" Noah asked.

"Naw! I ain't neva seen him, bro."

Kevion was just sitting there looking as if he was in deep thought. *Yo brother gon' be next,* kept ringing in his head.

"Let me see that phone," Kevion told his brother.

"Yo, I already checked it and the last call that came through was from a "B. Boy"," Devion said.

"B. Boy?" TK said out loud. "B. Boy? You think that stand for Big Boy?"

"You talking about Big Boy that sloppy fat ass nigga on the other side of town that don't wanna get down with the program?" Kevion asked.

"I don't know, bro, but we need to find out, though. But thinking about it, it could be him. I know his ass ain't making the cheddar he used to make since we got most of D-Town on lock," Devion said.

Kevion grabbed the phone and dialed the last call that came from B. Boy.

The person on the other end answered, "Yo Rasta what's good, baby? You knocked off that bitch ass nigga already?"

"Naw bitch ass nigga, but I'll tell you what, Big Boy, I'm going to give you a chance to let your mom see you one last time, Because I promise you, it won't ' be an open casket funeral if they find you at all," Kevion said with deep hatred in his voice.

Without saying another word Big Boy just hung up the phone.

As Kevion hung up, Devion asked, "Yo, that was him? How you know it was Big Boy?"

"I didn't," Kevion said. "He told me it was him when he hung up in my face."

"Yo, that nigga got a couple spots ova in Red Bird," TK said.

"Alright look, Noah, call up the workers at the spots and tell them to be on point at all times. C'mon, everybody make sure y'all strapped tight. We are about to ride over there and see if we can catch him slipping. He's nervous right now, so he can't think straight. He's bound to pop up on the streets because he's probably too paranoid to stay in one spot," Kevion said.

Devion came from the back room with three AK 47's and a couple of AR 15's. "Y'all put these in y'all car," Devion said.

Devion checked on Honey to make sure she was okay. After easing her nerves and reassuring her that everything would be fine, he told her to stay in the house and wait for him to come back. She had proven that she was loyal to him, so he was not reluctant about leaving her there alone.

As Devion made his way out the door, Honey said to him, "Alright Daddy, be careful and hurry back to me, my love."

# Chapter 14

The crew had been posted up for about forty-five minutes in positions where they could see anything coming in or out of Big Boy's house when a black on black BMW 750Li zoomed past them and stopped in front of the house.

"You see this fat muthafucka? He think shit cool," Devion said.

"So what you wanna do, bro?" Kevion asked

"I wanna just run up in his shit and push that nigga edge up back, but ain't no tellin' how many other niggas up in there. So this what we gon' do. We gon' wait till we get that fat bastard out in the open. Since I know he ain't gon' let his goons leave him, we gon' kill them first, ya dig?" Devion replied.

Kevion sucked his teeth and said, "I don't wanna kill big boy right off. I wanna bring him to the spot and watch him suffer."

"Yo, Noah," Devion said into the phone. "As soon as he leave and make it down the block, I want y'all to block him in from the front and we gonna come up from the back. If they get out bustin', dump on them, fuck it, but I do wanna bring Big Boy in alive, if possible."

"A'ight, family, I got you," Noah said.

Since TK and JoJo were behind Devion and his brother, they would come from the back as well.

Twenty minutes later, Big Boy came out of the house and jumped into his car by himself.

"Damn, he just gon' make dis shit easy, huh?" Devion said.

As soon as Big Boy made it down the block away from the help of his goons back at his trap, Noah and Curtis pulled out in front of him, making him come to an abrupt stop. Big Boy was unaware of the setup, and jumped out of his car, prepared to talk shit and ready to smack whoever it was that almost made him wreck his car.

With a pistol in hand, Noah jumped out the passenger side door and shot Big Boy in the leg, causing him to scream and drop down to his knees. Noah grabbed him by his collar and dragged him into the backseat of the car, jumping in with him. He took away the pistol Big Boy had tucked in his waistband and then placed it to his dome. After they had gotten him in the car, they drove off with the rest of the crew following behind.

"Yo, where we going?" Curtis asked Devion on the phone.

"Take that bitch ass nigga to the house," Devion ordered.

Then he made another call.

"Hey, baby girl, do me a favor and go into that back room down the hall to the left. And don't come out until I come in there and get you," Devion told Honey before they made it back to the house.

Not long after the call, they arrived at the safe house. Curtis and Noah dragged Big Boy and his bloody leg into the house. It also appeared as if he had gotten some nose work by the butt of Noah's gun. His nose had been broken on the bridge and had an ugly cut that poured out blood.

As soon as he made it into the house, Devion gave him a wicked body blow to his stomach which made him growl in pain. Big Boy went back down to his knees and was met by Kevion's Polo boot to his face.

Spitting out blood and grabbing at his stomach, Big Boy begged for his life with a promise to leave town.

"Oh, yo punk ass want mercy, huh?" Devion asked Big Boy.

"Yes, please have mercy on me, you'll never see me again," Big Boy said.

"But if it were up to you, we wouldn't have gotten that treatment," Devion said. "Hell, ya boy Rasta almost pushed my shit back earlier. I didn't hear him give me the option to live or die. As a matter of fact, you wanted us all dead."

With that, TK hit him so hard in the mouth that Big Boy spit out two of his teeth.

"Yo, go grab some rope from the garage and tie his fat ass to the chair," Devion said.

Turning back to their prisoner, he said, "You just couldn't get with the program, huh Big?"

"Nigga, you think you could take down The Love Boys, fat ass nigga?" Kevion spat. "Because of your dumb ass, now your whole family is gonna suffer. Bitch made ass nigga."

Taking a pair of pliers, Devion held open Big Boy's mouth and grabbed his tongue pulling it forward. Then with his butcher's knife in hand, with one slice, he sliced his tongue out of his mouth, throwing it to the ground.

JoJo stepped on it, then spit in Big Boy's mouth.

"Since you don't wanna talk about what we talking about, now you ain't gotta say shit," JoJo said.

Then suddenly, he lifted the gun and with a single bullet, Kevion put one in Big Boy's head. *That's for trying to kill my brother*, he thought.

"Damn! Crazy ass nigga! I hope the neighbors didn't hear that shot go off," Devion said. Then he went into the backroom to see if Honey was straight.

"You get 'em, baby?" Honey asked with excitement.

"Yea, we got him, baby, but we ain't done yet," Devion said while grabbing her and looking into her eyes.

He was fully acknowledging that if it hadn't been for her, he wouldn't be here. Grabbing her ass, he kissed her in a way that he never kissed her, a soft, but deep kiss. Then, he left her in the room and walked out to see his brother hanging up the phone.

"Yo, everybody straight and know what the fuck is going on?" Devion asked walking back into the room.

"Yea, Nick and his goons are on their way over," Kevion said.

"Ain't no use in sending family members any body parts," JoJo said.

"No, we just gonna have Nick and his boys pick him up and drop his ass at the pig farm. Ain't gone be no funeral, Trick!" Devion spat at Big Boy's lifeless body.

Once the body had been picked up, The Love Boys and their crew headed back to Big Boy's spot. The came up with the plan to send a couple of Nick's goons to act as if they were customers, knowing that no one would recognize them since they weren't from the same hood. When Big Boy's workers came out the house, JoJo and TK bum-rushed the door, sending a bullet through the doorman and watchman who sat in a chair close by the door. The other cats didn't have time to draw their pistols before they had pistols pointed at them. Then Kevion and Devion entered the house and ordered the killing of all the remaining workers. Before leaving, they gathered the drug supply just for good measure.

Once they made it back to the safe house, Devion used his brother's car to take Honey to her house. He left her with instructions to watch the news and see if the law was looking for them.

□

# Chapter 15

Honey called Devion early that morning and let him know that the cameras at the Waffle House weren't working and there were no witnesses who were willing to come forward and ID them or tell the police anything.

"Are you positive, baby girl?" Devion asked Honey.

"Yes, baby. I looked at the news all night and the incident did make everybody's news, but they didn't have anything," Honey said.

"Cool," Devion said. "So check it, I'm going to come scoop you up after I get me some shut eye, ma. Just take ya time and relax for the day, shawty. You had a hell of a day yesterday, don't you think?"

"Yes, I'm not in a hurry to get my car or anything, but I just keep thinking back to how I almost lost you, babe, and I really just wanna be with you right now," Honey said.

"I feel you on that, shawty. A'ight, give me a few hours and I'll be ova, but don't trip if I'm falling asleep on your ass, lil momma."

Laughing, she said, "I won't, I just wanna be around you, that's all."

"And no freaky shit," Devion joked with a laugh.

"Umm, okay," Honey replied with a bit of sadness in her voice.

"What's that Umm shit?" Devion asked catching on to her sly reply. "I'm for real, I'm so tired I don't think he can work right now," Devion said playfully.

Honey said nothing at first, but then she said, "Okay baby, just come on over." But in her mind she thought, *Shit, I bet I can bring him back to life.*

"A'ight, I'll hit you when I'm outside," Devion said with a coy smile.

"Okay," Honey said, then they both hung up.

*****************************

It was twelve o'clock when Kevion received a call from Duran. Devion had already left again and Duran was calling to inform them that he had gotten word back already about opening those businesses.

Kevion didn't tell Duran about the assassination attempt because they had everything under control. Kevion only gave Duran the addresses to the buildings he wanted for the businesses and he and Duran also set up another delivery for that weekend.

It was already Tuesday, but it was more than enough time to get rid of the remainder of what they had left in storage, even with the two days they basically had taken off to take care of Big Boy and his crew.

Taking the day off as well, Kevion arranged for Hershey to come over. Since she didn't have to go to work until that night, Kevion felt the need to take some of his frustrations out on Hershey's fat, juicy, and tight twat.

When Devion made it back to the house after taking Honey back to get her car, he and Kevion went for a drive. Even though the workers and the crew were off, the Love Boys got back out in the street, just to feel and see how the streets were shaking and moving. They weren't out for business right now, but they ran into a few cats they knew, and they set up business arrangements for the next day. They cruised the streets all night, talking and planning on how they needed to tighten up.

Kevion also expressed how he was grateful for Honey being where she was and doing what she did.

"Yo, bro, you got a down ass female on your side, son. As far as I'm concerned it doesn't get any more loyal than that. I'm cool if you want her to come to the pad and shit," Kevion said.

"Yea, she straight and I'ma tell her what you said, but I'm focused on getting this paper so I can get me a big ass crib to bring her to. That was straight love, what she did. Anyone of them other chicken head ass hoes probably woulda' let a G get smoked. She stay down like she do and don't flip the script, I don't know. I'll probably pump a few seeds in her and see what I come up with, feel me?"

"Yea, I feel you on that, bro. We just gotta stay focused so when the day comes, our females and kids won't want for nothing." Kevion paused. "I almost forgot, Duran hit me up earlier with some good news on the legit businesses we been thinking about," Kevion continued.

"What he say?" Devion asked.

"He basically just told me that the shit was a go and he took down the addresses of the spots so he could get the paperwork done."

"You tell him about Big Boy and shit?"

"Naw, bro, we handled that so it wasn't anything to tell, feel me?"

"Yea that's exactly what I was thinking," Devion said.

*******************************

The next day, it was back to business with the workers manning their positions at the traps. The crew handled all the big business that needed to be taken care of. Finishing up from grinding around six thirty Kevion and Devion went to their grandmother's house to have dinner with her and Uncle Cameron since he was still in town. He had been home for a week now since the league was in off season. He still maintained a house in the Dallas area to keep an eye on his nephews when he was not playing professional football.

While on the way to the house the Love Boys decided to swing by one of the traps and stay for a while, just to make sure things were running smoothly and to take a load off the workers' hands for a few hours. This was something they did from time to time, so as to not forget where they came from.

With an old school Thug Motivation 101 by Young Jeezy pumpin' through the speakers, the crew ground it out till four in the morning. When things started to get slow, they had a lil bit over two ounces left at fifty-nine grams. The way the trap was moving, they would be out by Friday night which was right on time for the next shipment.

The Love Boys left the workers to finish up the night, letting them know they could close shop for the morning, but to be back open no later than one that afternoon. If it was worth it, the smokers knew how to get in contact with the workers so no real money would be lost.

The week came and went, but on Friday, Cleopatra called Devion and told him that he and his brother should meet them for dinner at Benihana at seven. After the boys had dressed to impress, they rode in separate cars to the dinner meeting, arriving to find Cleopatra and Zolandria both waiting at a table in the back of the restaurant.

"Ladies," the boys said in unison.

"Good evening, gentlemen. How are you two doing?" Cleopatra asked

"We good, ma, thanks for asking," Kevion said.

"So what do we owe the surprise of you two meeting us outside of business, hours?" Devion asked.

With a light laugh, Cleopatra said, "With us, it is always business, Papi, and gave him a wink of the eye.

After sitting down and ordering, Cleopatra produced two rings that both had six keys on them and placed them in front of the Love Boys.

"And what are these for?" Devion asked.

"Why, dem your new building keys, gentlemen," Zolandria said.

"The buildings were purchased the other day and we got the keys this morning," Cleopatra said smiling with her million dollar smile.

"The paperwork has been taken care of already, so now all you two have to do is give the contractors the plans for what you want them to do, so they can get to work. Here are their cards, so you can set up a meeting with them sometime next week. You boys think a lot like your father because he built and maintained five Massage Parlors in three different states. Since he's been in, Zolandria and I are the ones who make sure that the businesses run smoothly."

Zolandria picked up the story. "All da women who worked for him on da street are now licensed masseuses, who your father has put through school to run a "somewhat" legitimate business. He figured, why let da Chinese get all da money in der undercover prostitution operation."

"Aww, that's some smart shit!" Devion said enthusiastically. *Damn, why didn't I think of that? I could put Honey in the joint with a couple of her girls and make a killin!* Devion thought.

Taking the business cards and keys, Kevion thanked them and told them to be sure to tell Duran that they appreciated all that he'd done.

Their dinners were prepared on the Hibachi Grill before them and they all ate different types of steaks with salads, capped off with a few drinks.

While talking, they agreed to meet at the warehouse at two in the afternoon the next day.

Zolandria had one too many drinks. Devion could tell by the way her eyes drooped and the slight slur in her speech which was difficult to comprehend even on her most sober days. Although he had to admit, that Jamaican accent turned him on in ways he never imagined. Since she sat next to him, he grazed the skin right behind her lower ear with his fingernail just to see if she would resist.

His delicate touch sent chills up her body as she closed her eyes and enjoyed the slight pleasure.

"Don't start nothing ya can't finish," Zolandria said teasing Devion.

"Is that a threat?" he asked whispering into her ear.

She just smiled. "Can ya take me home and make sure I get der and tucked in safely?" she asked.

Without hesitation, as Devion stood up and helped Zolandria out of her chair, he said, "Hey, we 'bout to be out. I'll see you at the house bro and Miss Cleo I'll see you tomorrow."

"Hey, bro, be on your shit," Kevion told Devion to remind him that slippers count and that he had to be safe.

"Hey, Cleo, I'll see ya in da morning," Zolandria told her.

"Alright girl, enjoy your evening, mami," Cleopatra shot back.

Pulling out of the parking lot Devion asked his inebriated passenger, "Which direction am I going?" Zolandria replied talking a little slower than usual. "I stay downtown at **The W**."

Devion had heard of the lavish condos offered in The W, but he had no idea his pops was providing this type of lifestyle for his women. The car was fairly quiet during the short drive to downtown Dallas. Zolandria was lying back in her seat, feeling the wind on her face from the opened sunroof top. Once they arrived and the doorman took the keys to park the car, they headed for the elevator. Shortly after the elevator door closed and Zolandria hit the button for her floor, they attacked each other, engaging in tongue wrestling and spit swapping. Even stepping out of the elevator on the fourteenth floor, they continued to kiss down the hall until she made it to her door, stopping long enough to retrieve her keys and unlock her door.

Once Devion stepped in behind her and closed and locked the door, he grabbed and pulled her closer to him with one arm and the other he dropped over her shoulder. His fingers traveled down her blouse and then searched under her bra for her already erect fat nipples. He kissed her neck behind her ear while licking her ear lobe.

As he squeezed and flicked her nipple, she leaned her head back and released a slight moan reacting to the tender wet kisses he planted on her.

Regaining her composure, she pulled away from him telling him to hold on while she slipped into the bedroom to get out of her clothes and into something more comfortable.

While Devion sat and waited on her couch, he pulled out his stash of coke and made him a few lines on her coffee table. Before he could finish his last line, Zolandria appeared in the doorway wearing Victoria's Secret lingerie: a pair of white see-through Brazilian cut panties with a matching bra. Since the lights were dim, her dark oiled skin illuminated off of the moonlight that shone through her window.

Devion noticed that she also wore a pair of white fluffy house shoe pumps which made the well-toned muscles in her legs flex.

With a finger, she told Devion to come to her. After he had done the last line, he rose from his seat and walked to her. While walking toward her, he took off his Armani shirt and tossed it to the floor, revealing his muscular and tattooed upper body. When he got within inches of her, he stopped and just took in this Jamaican beauty who stood before him.

She kissed him and rubbed between his legs, finding his penis already at full attention. Rubbing it gently, she backed away leading him toward the bedroom. Even as she moved, she unbuckled his belt and unbuttoned his pants. He took his two chrome forty-fives out before they hit the floor and placed them on the nightstand.

While she laid on the silk sheets of her bed, Devion reached behind her and undid her bra with one hand like a playa was supposed to, releasing and revealing her caramel brown voluptuous breasts. Her dark brown nipples were already erect. Laying down next to her, he put one of her nipples in his mouth, sucking on it softly while grabbing and squeezing her other full breast. He licked down her chest all the way to her navel and back up finding her mouth once more.

*This here is Pops', so I'm going to leave the taste of the pussy to him*, Devion thought.

Zolandria stroked his dick and squeezed his balls just right and grazed his nut sack with her perfectly manicured nails. That turned him on and he went in search of a condom.

Since he always had some stashed in his wallet, he had a few on deck and gave one to her to put on him. While he came out of his boxers, he laid down on his back, his dick standing straight up like the Eiffel Tower. Before she put the condom on, she placed one of his nuts in her mouth and sucked on it gently while stroking the head of his penis.

It felt so good to him, it sent a shiver up his spine and for a brief second eased his mind.

She licked the belly, then went back to his penis and sucked on his head. Zolandria took pride in her head game and gave Devion some of the best head he had ever gotten.

Devion still had complete control of his body and only nutted when he was ready. Once her jaws became sore and numb from giving him oral pleasure, she took the condom out of the wrapper and put it on him with her mouth. That was something no female had ever done with him before.

She stood up, pulled her panties down and stepped out of them one leg at a time. She squatted down like she was doing squats and guided his penis directly into the walls of her pussy. Still in a squat position, she rode up and down on the blessed piece of wood, he was blessed with, stopping each time at the top to squeeze her walls, and gripped his head.

Devion leaned up and placed one of her breast in his mouth and sucked it while she gyrated while going up and down until her legs grew tired. He flipped her over and she got on hands and knees and he penetrated her from behind.

Grabbing her dreads like they were reins on a horse, Devion pulled while giving her long powerful strokes that made her ass jiggle as if it was a wave in the ocean. He smacked her a few times and if someone had been in the other room, they would have mistaken all the smacking noise as something from a Bruce Lee flick.

After a few hours of lustful lovemaking, Devion got up without saying a word, took a shit, a hot shower and then got dressed. He grabbed his two pistols from the nightstand and left.

Since he knew her loyalty and dedication was to his ole' man, there wasn't any use of having small talk and arranging for her to be put into his stable because this wasn't nothing but a fuck thing.

Zolandria enjoyed her romp with Devion, but she was on the same page as him. After Devion had left, she took a long hot shower before heading to bed. She went to sleep knowing that she had to be up early the next morning to get the shipment and deliver it to the Love Boys and crew.

# Chapter 16

Kevion was awakened by the sound of his cell phone ringing, early that morning. It was 8:30 and Xavier was in his ear. Xavier would have been their major competition in the city, but they had been boys since Xavier's mom married into the family 15 years ago. Instead of being crosstown rivals, they were cousins who just happened to both be in the drug game. Xavier and his crew held it down in Fort Worth and the Love Boys took care of Dallas.

"Hey wake up, G," Xavier said.

"What's crackin' cuz, tell me something good," Kevion said.

"Yo, I gotta take a trip out to Cali later today and I think you and Devion need to roll with me. One of my partnas wants to holla about something major," Xavier said.

Knowing that Xavier was all business, Kevion knew the trip would be about some big chips, so he said, "A'ight, go ahead and include me and my bro when you get the plane tickets. Do we need to pack anything?" he asked.

"Naw, you straight, we should get there no later than seven and be back on the plane by eleven."

"A'right family. We have some business to handle first so we will hit you up this afternoon. Text me and let me know what time the flight will be leaving."

"A'right, cuz. I'll lace you up on everything once we get on the plane," Xavier replied.

Kevion got up to get a glass of strawberry-orange juice when he saw his brother watching at Sports Center, with the television on mute, while the classic song "High Life" by the group UGK, played through the speakers of their surround sound system. He was smoking a blunt with an empty plate in front of him and a half-empty bottle of Corona beer sitting on the table.

"What's up, bro?" Kevion said since Devion had his back toward him as he sat on the couch.

"Hey, what's good, bro," Devion shot back. "It's some waffles, eggs, and sausage in the oven, bro if you want it."

"Damn! Lil momma put that whipping on you like that, son? Got you whippin' up breakfast for a gangsta and shit," Kevion said laughing.

"Naw, partna, ain't no shit that good gonna have a playa like me whipped, nigga. You know betta than that," Devion shot back.

"So, you did hit that?" Kevion said.

Devion, realizing he just got tricked into telling his business, shot back, "Slick ass mufucka, you fuckin' right I tapped that ass. Took a shit and left," Devion told him.

Kevion busted out laughing. "You'z a crazy muthafucka. Yo, you be on some wild shit, family, but tell you the truth, I probably woulda done the same shit, bro." Kevion disappeared into the kitchen and warmed up his plate while fixing the glass of juice he came to get.

"You wanna hit this shit?" Devion shouted.

"I'm straight, bro, but roll another one up so I can fire it up after I finish eating," Kevion replied.

"It's already one in the ashtray," Devion shot back at him.

Kevion peeped his head out the kitchen and said, "Yo, before I forget, Xavier called and wants us to roll to Cali with him today for a business deal. He said he will fill us in on the details later. He is getting us plane tickets for later today. It will be a turnaround trip, so there's no need to pack anything."

"Cool," Devion replied.

Like Kevion, he knew Xavier was all business and about that cash. If he was calling them in on something it was legit and there was no need to ask a lot of questions beforehand.

After getting dressed and leaving the house together in Devion's car at 1:30, they made it to the warehouse in just ten minutes, right before everyone else got there. Once everyone arrived they unloaded four hundred kilos of product from Cleopatra and Zolandria's truck. Two hundred keys of coke and two hundred keys of heroin.

The traps were moving more than one kilo and a half of dope a week. So Devion gave two keys a piece to the workers to go to both spots.

Devion and Zolandria acted as if they had not just gotten their fuck on a few hours before, and just greeted each other before they each got to work unloading the truck and storing the product in the warehouse.

After everyone had left, Kevion checked his phone and saw he had a text from Xavier that said their flight would be leaving at 5:00. They locked up the warehouse and headed for the airport.

******************************

Once they boarded the plane with Xavier and his right-hand boy, Marcus, Devion was the first to speak.

"Say X, so what's the deal with these muthafuckas?"

"Money, bro," Xavier answered. "I met them a while back. They some ese' cats up in LA that be fuckin' with major weight. I told them that y'all are now supplying the Dallas/Fort Worth area with your new Cuban connection. They've always just bought ten keys of coke from me every week, and now they see we ain't bullshitting with the flavor so they are ready to upgrade. Ya dig?" Xavier said.

"You got any idea on what they trying to upgrade to?" Kevion asked

"Yea, they already told me if it's the shit, then they want to increase their quantity of Cocaine and include Heroine into their order. They estimate they would need 100 keys of each per month. Real talk."

Kevion did the math in his head and thought, *damn, twenty-four million is a nice piece of change to be making every month for a year. That'll be two hundred eighty-eight million.*

"You already did the background on them, bro?" Devion asked.

"Trust me, they straight. I did the background before I started supplying them and some of my boys been fuckin' with them since they got out of high school and jumped off the porch. His name is Juan, by the way, and the cat use to stay in Dallas back in the G. All they wanna do is meet the crew and set up plans on how we gon' transport all their shit and exchange the money. They already got a pilot that'll come pick it up with a couple of workers, but like I said, they just wanna meet the crew and make sure we can handle this order on a consistent basis."

"I can respect that," Kevion said "Shiiiit. I'd wanna meet whoever gonna be getting 24 million of my dollars, too."

Each of the crew ordered drinks once the plane reached the cruising altitude, but they all only had two drinks, just enough to take the edge off, relax and enjoy the rest of the flight.

Kevion had initially thought about flying in their dad's private jet but decided otherwise. He wanted his crew to know that he was still a street nigga. A hungry street nigga at that.

*How was that ass last night, son?* The text in Devion's phone read.

Devion shook his head and texted back: *Damn, how you know, Pops? I wanted to be the one to tell you.*

Derry Don sent: *LOL, son, son, son who you think sent it to you? After she told me you tried to get that ass when you first met, I told her to go ahead and give you a lil pussy. But check it, we can talk bout all that when y'all come up here to visit.*

*A'ight pops that's a bet. The Crew on our way to Cali on some business so I'll hit you up when we make it back.* Devion texted.

*Make sure you two watching each other's back and be safe*, Derry Don texted.

*A'ight Pops, One.*

Once they landed and made it off the plane, at curbside, there was an all-white limo waiting for them. The Hispanic driver held up a sign saying, **"The Love Boyz."**

They greeted the driver and then all piled into the car. Once they made it out of LAX, they were taken to Juan's summer house up in the hills. When they arrived, they were escorted to a large living room and the same limo driver offered drinks which they all refused.

The driver said, "Mr. Juan will be with you shortly."

After only a minute of waiting, Juan came walking through, wearing an all-white linen pantsuit with white sandals. He wore a platinum bracelet and watch. Juan was average height, maybe 5 ft 10 with a medium build and long hair that he had pulled back into a ponytail. Since he knew Xavier, he greeted him with a handshake. Then, Xavier introduced him to Kevion and Devion as the head of the crew.

They all shook his hands, then Juan sat on one of his leather chairs and grabbed a Cuban cigar out of the box on the coffee table. He extended the box to the crew, offering each one.

Xavier and Devion accepted the box, lit their cigars and inhaled the potent smoke.

"So how was the flight?" Juan asked.

"It was pleasant," Kevion spoke up. "I appreciate you for inviting us into your home, Juan, but let's get down to business," Kevion said letting Juan know right off the top, this was all business and no play with him and his crew.

Juan took a puff of his cigar, held it in for a few seconds and then blew it out.

"Ahh yes, business; well I'm pretty sure Xavier has already given you the numbers, so I just want your word that you can fill the order."

"Yes, that's no problem, Mr. Juan," Kevion said. "And I was also made aware that you would arrange to have it picked up, correct?"

"That's correct," Juan answered.

"Well if business runs smoothly as it should, I'll be willing to take ten grand off of every key as the business relationship progresses."

"Then it's a deal?" Juan asked.

With a shake of the hand, the deal was sealed with the first order to be picked up in a couple of days.

"What time does your flight depart?" Juan asked.

"In a couple of hours. Why?" Devion replied.

Juan took a puff from his cigar and after blowing a ring of smoke in the air, he said, "Well I could have my chef fix you all something to eat while we wait. Maybe we could have a few drinks and get better acquainted."

Kevion narrowed his eyes a bit and replied, "Thank you but no thank you on the food Mi' amigo. But the drinks we can do. You have Hennessy and Remy?"

The Love Boys were real particular about accepting food from just anyone. They could go with the drinks because they would be right there to see them being made, but trusting someone they didn't know with their food was a major faux pas.

While drinking and smoking cigars, Juan spoke of a few mutual acquaintances in Dallas that he helped get in on the dope game while he was living there. He also spoke of his family who was back in Mexico. He'd left his wife and two grown daughters there.

Even though Kevion didn't think he was young, he didn't think Juan was older than 45 being that he looked young. But his eyes and demeanor spoke and showed that he'd been around the block a few times, experiencing and seeing a lot in his day.

"So if you're from Mexico, how is it that you're not connected with the Cartel or Mexican Mafia?" Devion asked.

Kevion thought that was a good question and waited for a response.

Looking at Devion and puffing on his cigar, Juan said,

"I am very much connected with The Cartel, but with the position that I am in, I decide what I want to distribute to the streets. If business between us goes as smoothly as I plan, that would have been revealed to you in due time. See, the product that you have is the purest. Don't get me wrong, what we supply is pretty good, but what y'all have is better. See 400 kilos a month will turn into numbers you only dream of once the Cartel, my people, get their product directly from you," Juan said. "They are very much aware of the moves I'm making and the plans that I have in store."

Downplaying what Juan had just said, Kevion said,

"Okay, Mr. Juan, I hear you on everything you are saying and if we were to sell to you and your people, we would not only be very grateful, but I can tell you that we're very capable and will gain your trust and loyalty. But as for right now, I'm only concerned with the business at hand. You have my number, so call me and let me know where and when I can send someone to meet your pilot with the product so we can exercise our business opportunity. Thank you again for having us out here at your lovely home and I do appreciate your business."

Kevion rose from his seat and extended his hand to Juan for a handshake.

The crew started to head out the door since it was getting close to their flight time. They all shook hands once again, and then Juan ordered his driver to take the Love Boys and crew back to the airport.

Once on the plane, the crew talked briefly about what had transpired in the meeting. Then everyone, except Kevion, slept for the rest of the flight.

Kevion's mind was heavy. His father was locked away in prison, his mother was expecting another baby, his brother was almost assassinated, but the business seemed to be growing stronger and stronger, generating ridiculous amounts of money. He thought about everything his father taught him and said throughout the years. He thought about Juan again and wondered if his father would get in the bed with the Cartel knowing that those waters were always risky and deep.

One thing he did know about the Mexican Mafia and Cartels was that as long as you were about your business and no fuck boy shit, they could be some of the most loyal, people on earth.

# Chapter 17

That next week was a good week for the Love Boys and crew. They delivered as promised to Juan that Monday afternoon and business was moving as usual, even better that it was the first of the month.

Kevion and Devion had the contractors working on buildings, getting them up to code, painting, and adding the materials and furniture that was needed for each one. All of the businesses were expected to open in two weeks, so the Love Boys were excited to see how successful their new ventures would turn out.

Making good on their plans to hire from within their circle, they decided that their cousin Marco, who was a licensed barber, would be in charge of the new barber shop which they named **"Cut Boyz"**.

Koreana and Hannah, also their cousins, would be in charge of the beauty salon which they named **"Loving Hands Beauty Bar"**.

After careful consideration, they appointed TK and JoJo's younger brother Tre'Darion to run the club, named **"Club Love"**. He was calm, laid back and business minded. They knew he would keep a level head and ensure the club remained respectable and not draw any attention to their primary hustle.

After all, these were all positioned to be legitimate front businesses to wash their funds and substantiate the lifestyle and spending they were accustomed to living.

They visited their father that weekend and explained everything going on with Juan, the family, and the new businesses that were about to open. Devion and Derry Don joked about the sexual encounter he had set up with Zolandria. Their father expressed how proud he was of them, but stressed the fact that there was still a lot of work to be done and they needed to be especially cautious dealing with the Cartel.

They didn't tell their father about Big Boy; they knew he had enough on his mind as it was, and they didn't want him to be concerned.

***************************

Over the next several months, the Love Boys were successful in opening their businesses and increasing their presence in the drug game. One Saturday night, while out at their club, Kevion received a text message from Grandma Kristy saying that their mother had gone into labor and was on her way to the hospital.

"Yo, bro, the baby's coming," Kevion told Devion.

"Baby? Fuck you talking about, bro?" Devion asked not thinking about his mother's pregnancy since his mind was clouded by marijuana and alcohol.

"Crazy ass, boy. Momma's on her way to the hospital, bro," Kevion spat back, agitated as he headed toward the exit door.

Without another word, Devion jumped up from the couch in the VIP Lounge with a bottle of Remy in hand. He ran out of the club and jumped into the car with his brother.

At 2:26 that morning, their mother gave birth to a baby girl. She was named Marie, a name that came from Derry Don's little sister's middle name. Her full name was Marie Reshun Love Robinson and she weighed almost nine pounds and eight ounces.

When the Love Boys saw their mother in recovery after the delivery, they joked about the size of their baby sister.

"Must be all that protein, from peanut butter and tuna fish in your father's diet that he shot in me. She is a chunky little butterball!" Brandie joked and laughed.

With the thought of him, Brandie saddened and began to miss him more. Wishing that he was there with her for the birth of their daughter made her eyes swell with tears.

Seeing his mother's demeanor change, Kevion said,

"It's going to be alright, T-Jones; Pops will be out in a lil bit."

"Yea, I know; I just wish he was here right now, baby."

After those brief moments with their mother, the whole family from both sides came in to see Brandie and the baby. After making sure they were okay, everyone left so that Brandie could rest; they would all come back later on that day.

The Love Boys stayed the night to keep an eye on their mother and little sister. Primarily to make sure the doctors and nurses were doing what they supposed to.

The next day, Duran, Cleopatra, and Zolandria came walking into the hospital, bearing gifts for the baby and Brandie. Marie looked just like Brandie and was just as beautiful. She was cursed with her father's eyebrows, though. They were thick and bushy and were sloped, making her look as if she was mean mugging. With beautiful, thick and curly cold black hair, she had small feet like her mother and big hands like her father.

"How you feeling, mami?" Cleopatra asked.

"These drugs they got pumping in my IV don't have me feeling too much of anything." Brandie laughed.

All three women were laughing, showing their diamond grills.

"Chica, I know what I mean," Cleopatra said.

"I'm good. Even better now since I don't have to carry little momma's fat ass in my belly anymore," Brandie said.

"Ohhh, I'm going ta tell Derry Don ya called his little girl fat," Zolandria said jokingly.

"Please don't tell that man that. He was protective enough of his big headed boys. I already know you ain't gon' be able to tell him shit about his lil princess."

"Speaking of him, have you talked to him?" Duran asked.

"Yea, he called this morning, excited about me having a little girl, telling me how now he's gotta buy bigger and more guns. He was upset that he couldn't be here, but at least I sent him a picture of her on his phone. We talked for a long time this morning."

"Damn, I'm glad he has that cell phone in there. Those fifteen minutes calls he used to have just wasn't cutting it." Duran laughed.

Kevion and Devion said their goodbyes to everyone, telling their mother that they would be back later. Right now, they had business to take care of. Some of their high dollar customers were coming to pick up their usual orders, so the twins needed to get to the house, shower and change clothes.

After they had met the crew at the warehouse, they loaded up their cars with the product and drove to the private airstrip where Juan's plane was waiting. After making the exchange, they returned to the safe house to put the money up in the safe before Kevion and Devion decided to go by the trap house in Highland Hills. Passing by the Fire House on Bonnie View, they noticed SWAT and DEA gearing up.

Having a bad feeling, Devion called the workers at the house and told them to pack everything up and activate 'Code Black.' "We'll meet you there," Devion told them. In response, the workers quickly gathered the product and went ten houses down to the prearranged spot. It was the home of the Love Boys neighborhood surrogate mom, Momma Faye.

The Love Boys made it to Momma Faye's first with the workers pulling up just minutes later. Momma Faye's brothers were out in the front yard barbecuing, so the workers went inside while Kevion and Devion stayed outside. They stood outside to talk, but their primary reason was to watch their house.

As sure as shit stinks, the faggot ass laws hit the house. The twins were not concerned with being seen down the street because they knew the way search warrants worked. The cops would have only had a warrant for that particular property. Since the Love Boys knew that neither of them had outstanding warrants, there was no chance of the cops approaching them. Even if they were spotted.

"I bet they pissed," Devion said, sipping on a Corona. He laughed, as minutes later, the police came out of the house, frustrated.

"Damn, that was close," Kevion said out loud.

"Hey, bro, I already know you thinking it's time to move the operation, but let's move both spots at the same time, feel me?" Devion said.

"Yea, that'll be smart," Kevion said. "Matter fact, call them up over at the other house and tell them to pack everything up and meet us at the warehouse."

A few hours later, they all made it to the warehouse and stored the remainder of the drugs. Kevion told the crew that they were going to open up two new spots, but until then everyone could take some time off.

Between both of the houses, they had close to ninety thousand in cash and eighty-seven thousand in product.

"Hey, I'm going to come through and drop all y'all ten racks tomorrow," Devion said.

They were all grateful that they hadn't been caught in the spot; now it was time to regroup.

As soon as Kevion and Devion left, Kevion called up Ralph, a man they knew through their father who had real estate connections. He told him they needed two more spots and they wanted both that week. Kevion explained that they wanted one place in the Singing Hills neighborhood and the other in the Red Bird area. With this move, they would also put a stamp on Big Boy's old territory, which he chose to vacate when he made the costly mistake of putting a hit out on Devion.

"I got you," Ralph told Kevion. "I'll call you back in a couple of days so you can pick up the keys."

"Alright, that's a bet and yo! 'Preciate it," Kevion replied.

"No problem," Ralph said.

After taking care of all of their business, the Love Boys made their way back to their apartment ate, showered, changed clothes, then went back up to the hospital, bringing with them a plate from Boston Market for their mother since she'd called them complaining about the hospital food.

They both spent some time quality time with their little sister. Mostly just looking at her and touching her perfectly soft skin. She was only a day old, so the brothers didn't get much of a reaction from her, but they felt it was important for her to recognize their presence. They vowed to never let anything happen to their sister, as long as they were around. They didn't mention the near drug bust to their mom, so she was in a good mood as she began to devour the baked chicken, macaroni and cheese, and green beans that her sons had brought her.

After washing the first bites down with some sweet lemon tea, Brandie said,

"Hey boys, the hospital is releasing us tomorrow. So I'm going to need you two to come pick us up in the morning."

"Tomorrow? Why so early?" Devion asked.

"That's how they do now, baby," she said. "These damn hospitals don't keep women here no more than two or three days. As soon as everything's fine with the mother and baby, they try to get our ass up outta here quick."

"But is everything okay with you two, Momma?" Kevion asked.

"Yea, we straight. I got these stitches, but they'll heal. Your grandma is going to be at the house with me so we'll be okay, baby," Brandie said. "I'm ready to get my ass up outta here anyways, shit."

They all laughed.

"Hey, boys, I want y'all to know I love you two very much and I'm going to need you two to be careful and safe out in them dangerous streets. I want y'all's sister to grow up with two older brothers, so she'll have three men protecting her the same way y'all protected me."

"I love you, too, Momma," the boys said in unison.

"And you know we got each other out there, T-Jones," Kevion said.

"I know y'all do baby, just be careful and what I tell you about calling me T-Jones? Now you going to have your sister calling me that," Brandie said with a smirk on her face.

Both the boys burst out laughing and Devion said,

"Whatever T-Jones. You should be used to that name by now. Besides, we got it from our dad. He calls Grandma Kristy that all the time. Quit tripping."

After hugging their mother goodbye, the brothers jumped back into their car. As they were riding down I-75, Devion said,

"Say bro, all dis money we getting, why don't we get some laws on the payroll so we can know when they bitch ass coming?"

"I already thought about that D," Kevion said. "Those hoes can't be trusted, though. You forgot what happened to Tonk, bro?"

Tonk was a big time dealer from the Eastside, who seemed to have the control and protection of the streets. To everyone's surprise, his warehouse was raided and the feds confiscated so much product that it made national news. Tonk ended up getting sentenced to three life sentences in the federal penitentiary.

"Yea, I remember, but who knows why they set him up? He coulda stopped paying them or some crazy shit like that," Devion shot back.

"Exactly my point. Those hoes ain't never satisfied. We'll start off paying them, but it's only a matter of time before they are going to want more and more. Feel me?" Kevion said.

"I feel you on that, but we gotta do some'n, bro. We ain't gon' be lucky like that all the time. I'm glad we had the opportunity to warn them and I'm even mo' glad we went that way, 'cause if we hadn't seen DEA, we woulda' been up in that bitch waitin' when they got hit."

"Yea, that was a close call for sure," Kevion said.

His brother was right. *We gotta do something*, Kevion thought.

"Maybe it's time we upgrade our workers and give them a chance to make some real money with us," Devion said. "It ain't like we just met these cats; hell, we grew up with them in the same hood. We need to put the plans in motion so we can get out of the day to day operations. Like Duran, we can become the bosses who handle this shit from a distance."

Kevion thought, *Yea he just might be right with that.*

Devion continued, "We makin' million dollar deals, but we still taking thousand dollar chances."

"Alright bro, set up a meeting, they ain't getting no rings, just the chance to work with us. But let's go ahead and put them down. Instead of leaving them in those houses which are traps, we are going to give them a spot to stay at so they can get out of their mommas' house and on to some big shit."

Devion fired up a blunt. "A'ight, bro, let's have the meeting once we get the houses squared away, dig?"

"Right on," Kevion answered.

# Chapter 18

The workers that the Love Boys added to the crew, proved themselves to be very useful. With having more men roaming the streets, it gave Noah a chance to hit the highway, traveling to Louisiana, Atlanta, and Tennessee in search of new clientele.

Since the Love Boys had family in each location (Noah's mother was out of the ATL) they didn't have to go into any of these cities blind. Regardless if their family was in the game or not, they still knew what was what and who was who.

The new members of the crew were able to distribute some of the lighter weight to top hustlers and street hustlers, as well as make new contacts with heavy players in the game. Once the Love Boys checked out the background of the new customers, they set them up. The new contacts/customers were bringing in two million dollars every two weeks.

Seeing their pockets increase with cash only made everybody hungrier and focused so that they would stay on top of their game. Since Devion had put Honey in their club, he was also getting a lot more pocket change from her hustling skills as well.

The barber and beauty shops were the talk of the city, especially since they were more lavish than the competition, which caused the shops to be busy every weekend. Customers needed appointments if they wanted to be served.

On the personal front, Brandie and baby Marie were doing fine, with Marie getting bigger by the day. But the biggest change came with Juan. After nearly six months of supplying Juan and his crew, they were handling business and were now ready to expand their business – and start supplying The Cartel.

The Cartel was mainly based in Mexico, Miami, Arizona, California, and Texas. Juan came to Texas and met with the Love Boys at their safe house.

"I want you to know I am very pleased with how business has been going with us," Juan said. "Me and my people have talked and we think that it is time for us to make you our main supplier. Tell me, would you be able to guarantee us 50 tons each of heroin and cocaine every month?" Juan asked.

"That shouldn't be a problem at all," Kevion said while Devion couldn't believe his ears.

"Well, it's settled. I will set up a meeting next week so that everyone is on the same page and we'll iron out the details and numbers."

Since they'd known that Juan was coming to Dallas, and they knew his drink of choice was Tequila, Devion had purchased a bottle of the finest Tequila a day before and had it in the freezer. Kevion poured each of them a glass and they toasted to new opportunities. They sat and chatted about families and principles while they smoked Cuban cigars. A few hours later, Juan had his driver take him back to the airport, but he wasn't going home to Los Angeles. He was going to Mexico.

Once they were alone after Juan left, Kevion said, "Say bro, we got to make a visit to see Duran."

"Did that nigga just say 50 tons each?" Devion asked still not believing what he'd heard.

"Yea bro, the game has changed, my nigga. You can believe that," Kevion said.

"But, 50 tons! Gaaa Damn! And this nigga talking 'bout a monthly basis. Yo think we can handle that much weight consistently?"

"The way them fields look out there, I'm sure we won't have a problem. But we need to go holla at D to make sure that much weight can be delivered. We gotta have that connect, bro. We gotta make this shit happen, feel me? Niggas only get opportunities like this never in a lifetime, so we can't fuck this shit up."

"Call up Duran and tell him we on our way," Devion said, then paused as if he had another thought. "Matter of fact, you go holla at him. I'm going to stay here and make sure shit straight. It ain't like I'm missing shit anyways, so just fill me in on the details when you get back," Devion told his brother.

"A'ight bro, that's wuzzup. I'm going to leave in the morning, I need you to run by the club and holla at Tre D and scoop up the bread and deposit it in the bank. I'm going to swing by the shops and do the same. There's going to be a lot to discuss when I go see Uncle D, so I plan on being gone a couple of days." Kevion said.

"A'ight G, do what you gotta do to make sure everything straight, and I'm going to hold it down on this end. I'm 'bout to go and swing by the club and take care of this business, bro, then we can meet in the warehouse to pick up a lil sum'n for a few cats needing some work in the hoods and them broads need some boy out in the south," Devion said.

"Alright, since you are going that way, Nick and Loco need to re-up too, so hit them when you on your way over there so they can come pick up G," Kevion said.

"I got them, bro. After I finish up, I'll be at the crib unless I gotta get out. And you know I ain't coming out for no small piece of change. Shit, we lock them fifty tons down, we might as well leave everything under a key alone, unless we just supply the hood and just pick up money," Devion said.

*******************************

The next morning Kevion boarded his dad's private jet and headed to Cuba. On arrival, Senor Caja picked him up and took him to Duran's house.

"Hey, what's going on, nephew? What type of business brings you down here that we couldn't handle on the phone? Where's Devion? I assumed both of you were coming when you said that you were on your way." Duran asked greeting Kevion as he entered the house.

"Hey Uncle D," Kevion said while shaking Duran's hand.

"Everything's going good. Devion chose to stay home and handle some business that needed to be handled."

Then, he got right to business.

"Hey, Unc, remember me telling you about Juan out in Cali?"

"Yea, you talking 'bout the fella that's in the Cartel right? So what's up? There aren't any problems, are there?"

"Not the kind of problems that you would think. No," Kevion said.

"So what is it?" Duran asked.

"Well, he's setting up a meeting for us to meet with him and his Cartel family in a few days and they're ready to make us their main supplier," Kevion said.

"Well that's great! What type of numbers are they talking 'bout? I know the Cartel has money, so what are they going to need? One or two tons?"

Kevion laughed a little. "Try more like fifty tons, Unc, and that's each and every month," Kevion said, making sure he spoke clearly so Duran could understand him.

"And that's why I'm here. I wanted to see how we would transport all that weight and make sure we are able to supply them on a consistent basis."

"Oh yea, that isn't a problem but, damn! Fifty tons? That's a lot of dope son."

"Yea, I know..."

"But we got to make that happen," Duran said, cutting Kevion off.

"Yea, that's how me and my brother are thinking. So what are we going to do?"

"I'll tell you how we gon' handle it, we just gon' have to make as many trips necessary to fill the order and after three or so sales, we're going to have to buy a bigger plane, it's as simple as that. We could buy one now but let's make sure they're real about maintaining our business," Duran said.

"Okay, that sounds like a plan, so how's everything out here?"

"I can't complain, just enjoying life," Duran answered. He continued, "I see from the deposits you've made on the shops and club that everything is going as well as it should. I guess it's safe to say you and your brother made some smart investments."

"Yea, all the businesses are doing pretty good," Kevion said humbly.

"When your father hears this news, he's going to jump through the roof. I mean, we've moved a lot of dope before, but fifty tons to one buyer? Man! We didn't get lucky like that."

He paused and smiled at Kevion as if he were proud of him.

"But when you're on top of your business that's what happens. So how's your mom and Miss Marie doing?"

"They're doing fine and she's getting bigger by the day," Kevion said.

"From the pictures that I've seen, if that girl gets any bigger, it's going to be time for her to hit the weights," Duran said, and they both laughed.

"Yea, she's a pretty big girl," Kevion said.

"So when are you going to have an heir to your throne?" Duran asked.

Kevion was surprised by the question. "What do you mean?"

Duran grinned. "What you mean, what I mean? When are you going to have a few babies? If what I said at first wasn't clear enough."

Kevion chuckled. "To tell you the truth, Unc, that's nowhere near my mind right now. I'm concentrating on stacking this paper, so if I do decide to go that route, she or he or however many children I have, will be forever taken care of. Whether I'm here or not. Feel me?"

He nodded." Yes I do understand, but look, I'm not getting any younger and I would like to see you and your brother with a family of your own," Duran said.

"Matter fact, are you two still living in the same apartment?"

"Yes sir," Kevion said. "Why?"

"You two have a boatload full of money and I'm talking 'bout the Titanic. Why haven't you two bought or had a house built yet?"

"My brother has talked about it a time or two, but for me Unc, staying in that apartment humbles me and keeps me with an appetite if you know what I mean."

Duran paused as if he were considering Kevion's words.

"I like that, that's a good way to think." Then, turning back to business, he said, "So when is the next meeting with Juan?"

"He said it should be in a few days, but he's going to call me to set up a time and date."

"Alright, nephew, you know the game has changed. I'm sure and you gotta remember the Cartel is all about making money. But if you cross or betray them in any way, they will become ruthless. They don't just go after you, they go after anything and everything that means something to you. I've heard stories of them even killing the family dog."

"Yea, I know what they 'bout, Unc. But you know we all 'bout our business too, and we only killin' shit that try to fuck over us."

"Yea, I know, but I'm just telling you that you and your brother and the crew gotta be on your "A" game and stay on top of y'all shit," Duran said.

"Alright, Unc, I got you."

"So how long you planning on staying down here, my nephew?"

"I thought I would stay another day, you know. Hang out with you and hear some of those crazy stories you got about my dad. I know you got a lot of them."

Duran chuckled. "Stories? Hell, I can write a book on your old man by himself. We stayed in some shit coming up, finding our way."

He shook his head as if he were thinking about old times.

"Okay, let's go out and get some dinner. I know a fine restaurant not too far and we can swap stories over dinner. Just let me go throw on my jacket."

# Chapter 19

The Love Boys were on top of their game. Kevion and Devion had sealed the deal with the Cartel supplying them with their first shipment. The business with cats from out of state was growing and the legitimate businesses were doing great.

Everybody in the crews' family was taken care of and since Honey proved herself to be loyal and down for Devion, he bought a house and moved her in with him, leaving Kevion the apartment to himself.

The house he bought wasn't the big house he dreamed of having. It was a very modest 5 bedroom home with 4 ½ bathrooms, a 3 car garage and a gourmet kitchen on the 2nd floor. He had upgraded Honey's car and put her into a two-door Bentley coupe. For Devion, buying the house was just a test run, just to see how shit would turn out. He put Honey in charge of decorating; he just told her what colors he liked and wanted to see.

Honey was still on top of her game, working and hitting licks because she was not the type of woman to just sit on her ass and spend all of her man's money. She knew what she brought in was pocket change to Devion, but she still wanted to do her part. Besides, Devion wasn't going for that anyway. He did see himself having a child or two with her, but now wasn't the time. So he made sure to stay strapped when they had sex.

While dancing at the club one night, Honey was giving a trick a lap dance. The man who was high and drunk pulled his dick out and tried to pull her G-string to the side.

Before she had a chance to react, Devion was suddenly standing right over the trick with murder in his eyes. Devion was in the club and had seen the entire thing transpire. When the trick tried to stand up, Devion jabbed the man in the jaw so hard, it looked like his jaw came off its hinges and broke. Then, Devion took his pistol out and slapped the man on the bridge of his nose, causing blood to gush out. Even once the man was on the floor, Devion still saw blood red. He kept hitting him over and over, and would have killed him if Kevion hadn't pulled him off the unconscious trick.

With her sharp stiletto heel, Honey sent a single stomp to the left side of the man's face, punching a hole in his jaw. Her heel went straight through his skin and Honey had to pull and wiggle to retract her shoe from his face.

A couple of the members of the crew had to grab her and pull her back to stop her from kicking him again. Other members of the crew grabbed the man's unconscious body and dragged him out of the club. Then because he feared the man waking up and coming back, seeking revenge, Devion ordered his crew to get rid of him.

When his crew left with the man, the club returned back to normal and Devion allowed Honey to chill with him in the VIP lounge for the rest of the night.

"Hey, Daddy, I know you said I could take off for the rest of the night, but I wanna just chill for about thirty minutes. I'm okay now and I really wanna get back to work," Honey said.

"That's wuzzup, shawty. I can dig it. Have a couple of shots with me to not only calm yourself down, but me as well. I almost flashed out and killed that muthafucka in here with all those witnesses. I don't normally trip when niggas are touchin' or trickin' with you, but ain't nobody gon' be disrespecting my bitch. You know I got you, boo-boo, but what's understood don't have to be said."

Honey softly grabbed Devion's chin and looking deep into his eyes, she said,

"I know, baby. I know you got me and you know I got you, right?"

"Most definitely, baby girl." Looking at her smile at his answer and seeing her perfect white teeth, made Devion feel better already, and it gave him a thought.

"Hey, check this out, lady, my moms and a couple of my pops' chicks got diamonds placed in their teeth. If you were to get some, what color would you choose?" Devion asked Honey.

"Diamonds in my teeth? I never thought about that." She paused and grinned so that she could take a look at her teeth in the mirror wall behind the couch they were sitting on. After a moment, she said, "Damn that would be fly, Daddy."

"So what color?" Devion asked again.

"I don't know." She paused as she thought about it. "Powder blue always looks good on me," Honey said.

Devion tried to picture her smile with powder blue diamonds in her mouth. *Yea, she could rock that*, he thought in his head. Then, he said, "What about powder blue and pink?"

"Would you like that, Daddy?" Honey asked.

"To tell you the truth I think that'll look fly on you, shawty. We'll go holla at Dr. Ash tomorrow, and see wuzzup," Devion said.

"Okay, Daddy, I like the idea and if it makes you happy, you know I'm for it." Honey said.

They had their drinks and talked for a little while before Honey got up and went to go change into another outfit, leaving Devion sitting in the lounge by himself with a bottle of Remy on the table and a tray of coke.

Kevion walked into the lounge with a blunt hanging from his lips.

"You straight bro?" Devion asked.

"The question is, are you straight?"

"I'm good, bro," Devion said while reclining back in this seat.

"I seen you flash out in your eyes before you even made it to dude," Kevion said. "Honey was a damn fool with it, too. You see that hole she put in that nigga's face, bro?" Kevion asked.

"Yea, I think I'm in love," Devion said jokingly before they both burst out laughing.

"You's crazy, bro," Kevion said.

"Right on. Yo! Anyone of them niggas from the crew call and let you know if they handled that yet?" Devion asked.

"Naw, not yet." Then, a moment later, "Aww, shit, they walking thru the door now," Kevion said, seeing his members of the crew makin' their way back through the club.

When they made it to the lounge where The Love Boys were, the crew just sat down and started pouring up drinks as if nothing happened. Devion and Kevion knew they had some cold blooded killers on their payroll and they didn't even attempt to ask them a question that they already knew the answer to.

Enjoying the rest of the night, they smoked and drank talking about the business they needed to take care of the following week. Every member of the crew was getting paid, especially since they made that Cartel connect and all were planning on buying homes or condos away from the hood.

A few hours later, they all left the club. First Devion and Honey went home, and then, Hershey (who worked in the club as well) followed Kevion to his apartment to spend the night.

When they arrived at Kevion's apartment, Hershey took a shower to clean all the baby oil and sweat off her body. Then, she sat down on the couch next to Kevion.

"I have some news." She paused. "Baby, my period didn't come last week and I found out I'm pregnant," Hershey said.

"So what you tryin' to say, Hershey?" He didn't give her a chance to answer.

"As a matter of fact, congratulations, shawty. Who's the daddy? Do I know him?" Kevion asked.

"As a matter of fact you do," Hershey said with a smile.

"Who?" Kevion asked with a mixture of excitement and sarcasm.

"You, Papi," Hershey said.

"That's bullshit, girl, you trippin'," Kevion said looking Hershey dead in her face. "You high or something, shawty? You know I straps up all the time, baby girl. Why you coming at me like this? You blowing my high with this bullshit, ma."

Now, she wasn't so happy. "Oh, you forgot about that little situation about six weeks ago when we fucked," Hershey said.

"Six weeks ago?" Kevion said out loud, then went back to remember in his mind. He remembered that all three magnums from a box of rubbers, busted and broke every time, each one of them filled with semen oozing in her vagina.

"Damn!" Kevion said out loud.

"Oh, now you remember," Hershey said, pouting.

"Yea, I remember shawty," Kevion said with a smile on his face. "So what are we going to do about it, baby girl?"

"What you mean what we gon do about it? Negro, I'm keeping my baby regardless. If you ain't trying to take care of yours, I'm going to do it myself," she said with attitude.

"Shawty, I didn't mean it like that, baby girl. If it's mine, that ain't even a question if I'm going to take care of it, lil girl. My pops ain't turn his back on me or my brother, so I ain't turning my back on mine, feel me? I only asked what we gon' do because you got the ultimate say so in this. Regardless if I wanted to keep it or not, you decide if you get an abortion or not, shawty, so calm your little ass down, baby girl, and come here. Have I ever turned my back on you, Hershey?"

He wrapped his arms around her and she buried her head in his chest.

"No," she answered, in almost a whisper.

"So what would make you think that I would do that now, baby girl?"

"I don't know. I'm just scared and thought I would lose you because I'm pregnant, baby."

In Kevion's mind, he thought, *Damn, Uncle Duran done cursed my ass and wished this on a G.* But he smiled at the thought of raising his own lil shorty.

But while there was a smile on his face, he had thoughts in his mind. *Still gon' get that DNA, though. I ain't going out like Willie Lump Lump. Pops already told me how one of his chicks tried to get him before I was born.*

With that, a smile came on Hershey's face, and then she pushed Kevion back onto the couch, unzipped his pants, and let him enjoy the wetness of her pregnant pussy.

# Chapter 20

Early the next morning The Love Boys met up at the warehouse to let the crew get what they needed for the drops they had set up for the day. Kevion didn't tell his brother about the situation with Hershey because he didn't want to throw any of them off focus. He was only concerned about handling business, especially now that he needed to provide for the new member of the family.

Before everyone left, Kevion called a quick meeting with the crew.

"Since we have made a new, more upscale connection with the Cartel, my brother and I believe it's time for the whole crew to get sized up for tailored made suits. If we are going to make big money, we need to be dressed like money."

Kevion continued, "We decided that suits will be the official dress code for all major business meetings. Dressing that way will also show unity."

Some of the crew made fun of the idea but agreed to give it a try. They all jumped into two separate SUV's and drove to Kevion's personal tailor. Once they were fitted and saw themselves in those expensive suits, they liked the new look. Especially when they all came together – they all looked like a million bucks.

"Now you all look like gentlemen and about your business," Kevion joked.

"Ha! Ha! Ha! Very funny!" TK said.

After getting their suits sized and paid for, they all went back to the safe house. Upon arrival, Kevion ordered all of the top dawgs to sit at the large table. Everyone began looking around wondering what was about to happen next.

Kevion began walking around the table talking in a calm and steady voice.

"Check it, all y'all my niggas and you all have shown my brother and me that you are down for the cause. You have proven your loyalty to us on several different occasions. But I'm going to tell you all this one time and one time only. If this is not what you want for your life, you need to get your punk ass up and get the fuck outta my face ASAP," Kevion said looking into each crew member's eyes.

"I'm telling you, if yo' ass still around this table and in those seats, then the only way you getting out of this is through a pine box," Devion added.

With all of them wearing stern expressions, nobody even attempted to move.

"Nigga, this shit here is for life," TK said speaking for all of them.

"You fuckin' right this for life," Devion shouted.

With that, the Love Boys pulled out ring boxes and gave one to each member of the crew who they were promoting to top dog status. They placed the ring on the ring finger of their right hand, symbolizing that they were married to the game.

After the newly appointed top dogs finished admiring their rings, one by one they embraced the Love Boys to show their excitement about their promotion.

"A'ight, a'ight chill; this shit ain't ova just yet," Devion said smiling.

Devion went into the back room, then came out with a few duffle bags. He had to go to the back of the house three times before he handed each crew member their own bag, filled with a one hundred thousand dollar bonus.

Honey entered the room wearing a form fitting dress and smiling her new powder blue and pink diamond smile. She and Devion had gone to visit the dentist, Dr. Ash, earlier that week.

Right after she took a seat in Devion's lap, eight women walked through the hallway doorway and each one approached the new and original top dogs. They were dancers who worked in the club and once they were all in place, Honey pressed play on the entertainment center using the remote control. The rap artist, Twister's song, "Get It Wet" rang through the speakers while a hood flick that had been shot in various strip clubs appeared on the large flat screen.

"Y'all enjoy," Kevion said while rolling a blunt on the table that also held a bottle of Hennessy.

Noah went to the freezer and grabbed two large bottles of Cîroc, some diced pineapples and pineapple juice from the refrigerator. He placed them all on the table, poured a drink for him and his dancer while he put her to work to roll up more blunts.

This was exactly what Devion and Kevion wanted to see, their crew happy and made men. For the rest of the night, they partied, all enjoying themselves.

*******************************

The next morning, Kevion and Devion followed Noah and Nick to Atlanta to deliver 50 keys of cocaine. They traveled with them to not only protect the car with the dope in it from the state troopers, but they also wanted to go see Synthia, Noah's mom.

After they had met with the buyers at a remote location, they stopped by Synthia's crib. Noah wanted to lay some cash on his mom and sister, and at the same time, put some in a safe he had put in her house.

When they made it to the house and greeted Synthia, Devion noticed that she had diamonds placed in her teeth, just like Cleopatra, Zolandria, and of course, his mother. He knew she had them beforehand but this time he was connecting the dots and putting two and two together. Devion knew that when Synthia had met his father she already had gold teeth covering up damn near half of her teeth.

*But I guess this was Pops way of putting a stamp on it,* he thought.

"Hey, wuzzup, Momma," Noah said giving her a hug and kiss on the cheek.

"Chill'n. What's up with you? And why you didn't tell me you were coming this way? I could've had something to eat cooked or something," Synthia said.

"My fault, Momma, I really just came to bring you this," Noah said handing her a backpack with fifty grand in it.

"Where my sister at? I got something for her, too!"

"I sent her to the store a few minutes ago. She should be pulling up in a few since I just sent her to go get some milk, eggs, and beef tips."

Taking the backpack from Noah, she looked inside and her eyes got wide.

"What's this for?" she asked

"It's for you, for whatever you want it to be."

She grinned. "Okay, 'preciate it, baby," she said while putting the bag in the hall closet. But Noah knew she'd only put the bag there temporarily. His mother had her own safe in her bedroom and he was sure she'd stashed the bag in her safe once they left.

While Kevion and Devion talked to her, mainly talking about Derry Don, Noah went into his bedroom where he had a safe in the floor under his bed. It was hidden by the carpet. He opened the safe, put his money inside, and then went back into the front room. The twins and his mother were buckled over with laughter.

"What y'all laughing at?" Noah asked as he came back in the room. He noticed his sister in the kitchen and kissed her cheek.

"Man!" Devion began, barely able to talk since he was still laughing. "She just tellin' us how Pops shot himself in the foot one night on Uncle Cam's birthday coming from the club."

"Oh, yeah, I remember. Y'all's Grand-T was pissed about that!" Noah chuckled.

Noah turned his attention back to his sister, making small talk and giving her a necklace with a medium size heart to show how proud he was of her for finishing the naval basic training. He had gotten his hustling ways from his mom and had been in and out of trouble since he was 14 years old, but he was proud of his sister for doing the opposite. She managed to stay out of trouble, not get pregnant like a lot of girls in the hood and set positive goals.

They stayed with Noah's mother for just a little while longer before they said their goodbyes and headed back to Dallas. They'd been on the road for 10 hours and

were just about to come into Dallas on I-30 when an unmarked police car turned on their lights and pulled the car Kevion and Devion were traveling in over.

From the side view mirror, the brothers watched the officers approaching. Instead of officers in regular uniforms, these two were plain-clothes detectives, wearing jackets with brown patches on the elbows just like those old detectives on television shows. They approached the car from both sides.

While Kevion rolled down his window to talk to the officer on his side, Devion kept his tinted window rolled up prohibiting communication with the officer on the passenger side.

"What seems to be the problem, officer? I'm quite sure I wasn't speeding," Kevion said politely.

The detective on the other side tapped on Devion's window, then motioned for him to roll it down.

"No, there's no problem, Kevion," the officer said while looking into their vehicle. "No problem at all, Mr. Devion Robinson or Mr. Kevion Robinson. Or should I call you what the street calls you, The Love Boyz?"

"So what can I do for you, Detective?" Kevion said as he remained calm, cool, and collected.

"Just wanted to meet you two finally," the detective said, handing Kevion a card.

"What do I need this for?" Kevion asked, letting the card slip from his fingers and fall to the ground on purpose.

Picking the card up, the detective said, "Look here, you lil bastard, we can do this the easy way or the hard way. If you want everything to be smooth, you're going to have your black ass at the IHOP on Camp Wisdom at ten-thirty in the morning."

He threw the card in Kevion's window, then walked off.

"Have a good day," the other detective said following his partner back to their car.

Rolling up their windows and driving off, Kevion picked up the card: *Detective Corey Dotson.* That's all that was on the card besides a cell phone number underlined with black ink.

"What the fuck that shit all about?" Devion spat. "His bitch ass knew our government names and by sight at that."

"It was only a matter of time," Kevion said. "He don't want shit but a percentage, ya dig? You see them hoes didn't even search the car or us."

Devion's phone rang.

"Yea we straight, G," he said immediately. He knew it was Noah calling and checking in since he'd kept driving the other car when he saw them getting pulled over.

Kevion said, "Hey, tell Lil Noah to have everybody at the house within the next two hours."

"He heard you, G," Devion said hanging up the phone.

# Chapter 21

When everyone met at the house, they all sat at the table or on the sofas with a few blunts in the rotation. Kevion came out of the kitchen with a blunt in his mouth and a Corona in his hand.

"Look, family, I called everyone over here due to the new intelligence I just received. I just found out that one of the alphabet boys are on our shit."

Some of the crew moaned.

"Don't trip, though, because in fact, this could be a good thing for the team if we play our cards right. They knew our names and they knew us on sight, so I wouldn't be surprised if they knew all of y'all too," Kevion said. "So check it, he wants to meet with me and my brother in the morning and I'm confident that all he wants to talk about is how much money he can make off of our hard work. But, and this is a big but, if we get them on our team, I'm going to make sure we know what time it is with every agency on everything. It may sound crazy, but I was anticipating their arrival. I just didn't know when they were coming," Kevion said. "So dig, go home and enjoy the night and let us see what's happening in the morning and we'll know where to go from there."

"Man, this some fucked up shit. How you know they just want money and don't wanna lock us up?" JoJo asked.

"I don't know, cuz, that's why I don't want no business done until I meet with them to see what their angle is. But if they were tryna lock us up, they would have searched the car. So like I said, don't sweat it and I'll call y'all tomorrow to give you the okay to get back to business. Or if there's a lot to tell, I'll set up another meeting."

"A'ight family hit me soon as y'all done talking to them pigs," TK said getting up to leave followed by the rest of the crew.

"Alright family, I got you. I'll hit all y'all up in the morning," Kevion said.

When everyone was gone and he and Devion were alone, Kevion said, "Fuck!" and slammed his hands down on the kitchen countertop.

"What you tripping on, bro? It's a part of the game bro, and besides, if these bitches on that bullshit you know Juan and the Cartel muthafuckas love to kill pigs," Devion said.

"Yea, I know, but those bitches don't smell right. They smell of greed. And although we might get that protection, I can just imagine the cost we gone have to pay to have it, bro," Kevion said.

"Yea, I feel you on that, bro, but fuck, we gotta do what we gotta do to keep getting dis paper," Devion replied.

"Yea you right, D, I'll meet you in the morning bro, I'm about to go to the crib and chill. Everything at your spot straight? You and honey getting along bro?" Kevion asked.

"So far so good, ya dig? She keepin' me happy by any means necessary. Oh yeah, I heard it through the grapevine that Hershey pregnant and sayin' it's yours."

Kevion's eyebrows dipped in the way his fathers did, as if to say that was something he didn't wanna hear. He remembered putting off the conversation before appointing the new top dogs and with everything that had transpired, it slipped his mind.

"Oh, you heard that, huh?" Kevion asked.

"Yea, so what's up with that? You keepin' yo' brother in the dark now?"

"Naw, it ain't nothing like that, but check it, that's a whole 'nother conversation for another time. Let's handle the business we got to handle tomorrow and we'll talk about that later, straight?"

"Yea, bro. I'm 'bout to be out."

"Where you headed?" Kevion asked.

"Nowhere in particular, just 'bout to cruise the streets for a while before I head to the house."

Giving Devion some dap and a hug, Kevion said, "Alright bro. Stay on top and I'll see you tomorrow."

"Much love," they both said to each other at the same time.

******************************

The night came and went and Kevion was up extra early because he could hardly sleep that night. He called Devion to confirm the time they would meet that morning. He kissed Hershey on her forehead and stomach before heading out the door.

Kevion was already in IHOP's parking lot when Devion pulled up at 10:30 on the dot. Both dressed in designer suits, they got out of their cars and went into the breakfast diner. Right away they saw the two detectives sitting at the table waving at them.

Walking over to the circular booth the officers occupied, Kevion and Devion sat across from each other putting the detectives in the middle.

"Gentlemen, how are you doin'?" one of the detectives asked. But he didn't give the Love Boys a chance to respond before he continued. "As you already know, I'm Detective Dotson and that's my partner Detective Johnson. Would you two like a cup of coffee or anything?" Detective Dotson asked.

"Naw, I'm straight," Devion said.

"Hey, detectives, let's get to the point and please stop trying to act like we're all friends. What do you want?" Kevion asked.

"Kevion, Kevion, Kevion, look if I wanted to bust your ass, I could have done it already. The reason I called this meeting is because we would love for you to become best friends with us."

"And why would we do some shit like that?" Devion said.

"It's simple. Freedom and money," Detective Johnson said. "We can guarantee your freedom which would allow you two to continue in your operation and keep making money."

"So tell me something, Detective, how much is this so called protection gonna cost us?" Kevion said. "And how can you guarantee our freedom? I don't believe you work for all the law enforcement agencies."

The detective nodded as if he understood Kevion's point.

"Let me put it to you like this -- in every agency there is someone eager to make an extra buck, and it just so happens that I'm friends with those men in each agency. What we're asking for is a small fee to ensure your peace of mind."

Laughing, Devion said, "A small fee, huh?"

"So what's the small fee?" Kevion asked.

Detective Dotson took a piece of napkin and wrote on it, then slid it between the Love Boys.

"It won't go up and it won't go down. You can pay every two weeks."

Kevion grabbed and opened the napkin, then gave it to his brother.

"You already know what's next if you two decide to decline our generous offer," Detective Dotson said. "The first payment is already due. You two have my number so give me a call and we'll set up a drop-off site."

Then with a large smile Detective Johnson said, "Have a good day," before he ended the meeting, dismissing the Love Boys.

Without a word, Kevion and Devion got up from the booth and left.

"Meet me at the house," Kevion told Devion as they walked to their cars. "And call everybody and tell them to get back to work."

Devion followed Kevion back to his house. Once they got there, Kevion poured himself a glass of orange juice and sat down at the table with his brother.

"Since we put everybody back to work, I guess it's safe to say we gon' pay them dirty muthafuckas," Devion said.

"Two hundred and fifty racks bi-weekly or 500 thousand every month ain't too bad, especially when we can have all the law enforcement agencies in our hand. We gon' be straight bro, so let's just play our hand until we ready to throw it in and leave the game," Kevion said. "How much we got in the safe, D?"

"It's 'bout twenty-five mill in there, G. that we still ain't put in the bank yet," Devion said.

"Alright, let's get half a mill out, go put the rest in the bank, and gone and drop that off. Fuck all that meeting twice a month shit. I wanna see they bitch ass as little as possible, feel me?" Kevion said.

His brother nodded.

"Set up another meeting with the crew for tonight so we can put them on game."

"I got you bro," Devion said. "You think they mean what they say about not going up on the price?" he asked.

"Have I ever trusted the police?" Kevion shot back.

"Yea, I was thinking the same thing, bro. I might have to end up putting them in the dirt befor' all is said and done," Devion said.

"I hope it don't come to that, but they control they own destiny, bro," Kevion said.

# Chapter 22

"So Kevion, tell me, I hear you are having a little problem out this way," Juan said while picking up his order for the Cartel.

Kevion's eyebrow arched and he looked at Devion sitting across from him before he said, "Naw, there are no problems on this end, Juan. What are you talking about?"

Laughing, he said, "Listen there's nothing the Cartel doesn't know when it comes to the business. We hear you two have a couple of detectives dipping into your cookie jar."

"Like I said, there's no problem," Kevion said, knowing that he and his brother could handle their own issues.

"Well look, if you ever need a couple of rodents exterminated, I'm just a phone call away, okay?"

Kevion laughed. "Alright Juan, I got you, but I think we can control the situation. If anything changes, though, you will be one of the first to know about it."

"Okay Papi, you do that, because I'm very pleased with the business we're conducting and I can't afford to have two little money grubbing pricks interfering with it, understood?"

"Understood," Kevion said.

"Alright gentlemen, well I'll see you next month. You two stay on top and be careful," Juan said.

"A'ight G, you have a safe trip back to Mexico," Devion said.

After they had left the private airstrip, Kevion sent Noah to Nick's spot to deliver five kilos to him. Since he had opened another spot, he needed the extra two kilos instead of the regular three that he was moving on a consistent weekly basis.

Devion met one of his boys at the warehouse who brought a couple of his Louisiana kinfolk to give them three kilos to get rid of in the hood.

Even though the laws were dipping in the money, as long as business stayed straight, five hundred thousand a month was merely pocket change to the Love Boys and crew. Everybody still got paid the same, and the brothers had done that on purpose. Kevion figured the crew shouldn't have to suffer just because they had a fee to pay every month.

Once everyone was straight, Kevion went to check on their legitimate businesses. First, he checked in with their great aunt, Euree who had opened up the most recent business they had decided to open. It was an upscale dry cleaners which offered express spot cleaning and delivery services. They named the cleaners "**Clean With Love**". Their other great aunt, Patricia, who was a nurse, helped her little sister out at the cleaners whenever she was off or had time to do it.

Marco had the Barber Shop jumping and the Beauty Shop's business was growing daily.

"So what's going on Auntie?" Kevion said walking into the Dry Cleaners. He passed by the long line and since Euree was at the counter taking care of the customers, Kevion figured she was giving her employees a break.

"Business as usual," Euree said.

"And it seems that you have a lot of it," Kevion shot back. "You had any more photo shoots lately?" Asking his aunt since she was a model and he knew that was her first love.

"No, not yet, but I'm due to go to the Bahamas next week for a photo shoot. I'll only be gone for a couple of days and Patricia is going to run the cleaners since she's off those two days. Thank God."

"That's wuzzup. You make sure I get the new photos, lady."

"I got you, nephew. Have you seen or talked to your dad lately?"

"Naw, I haven't seen him, but my mom talks to him on the regular. We are supposed to visit him sometime this month, though."

"Well tell him I said Hi. I know he's probably feeling some type of way since I haven't written him back yet. He wrote about three or four months ago, but I've just been procrastinating on writing him."

"Alright Auntie, I'll tell him. Hey, I'm about to make a drop. You need me to do anything while I'm gone?"

"Yeah, give me a minute and I'll meet you in the office in the back. Let me get somebody up here to handle these customers."

Euree gave Kevion almost ten grand from the safe to drop at the bank as well.

After making the deposits at the bank, Kevion spoke with Hershey and agreed to take her for a doctor's appointment to check on their baby.

When he went to pick her up, the first thing he said to her was, "Why you opening your mouth and telling everybody your business, ma?"

"What you talking about, baby? I haven't been talking to no one about anything," Hershey said.

"Well, how does my brother know you're pregnant, shawty? Look, I ain't upset or no shit like that, but you know how I am about my business, baby girl."

"Baby, I only told Honey and she ain't gon' say shit to nobody. Hell, I thought you probably already told your brother."

"Naw, shit been a lil hectic on my end so I was waiting for shit to calm down before I told him. I didn't wanna put more on his mental than what is already there."

"Okay, baby, I'm sorry if I caused you any problems, but you know I got you and that I'm down for you through whatever."

Without saying another word Hersey unbuckled her seatbelt, leaned over, unzipped Kevion's pants and took Kevion's manhood into her mouth.

"You think you slick," Kevion said while gripping the back of her head and guiding her as he tried to force all of his manhood down her throat. "Don't try to right your wrongs now," Kevion said. But as he drove, he enjoyed the pleasure that she was giving him. She didn't stop until they arrived at the doctor's office.

It was a routine check-up and the doctor just made sure the baby was developing and getting the proper nutrients that it needed. Hershey got a prescription for prenatal vitamins and was told to put a halt to any smoking and drinking if she wanted to ensure a healthy baby and pregnancy.

Leaving the doctor's office, they first stopped at Cracker Barrel to get something to eat before Kevion dropped Hershey at her home. She had just gotten out of the car when his phone rang.

He glanced at the Caller ID, then said, "Hey, wuzzup Uncle D?"

"Nothing," Duran said. "Just calling to inform you that I purchased a bigger plane at a price that wasn't that bad. So now instead of making multiple trips back and forth, we have a plane that's capable of transporting the feed for the livestock in one trip. So look, you have one coming in tomorrow at noon. Have the crew there to meet it and help the girls unload and take it to the warehouse. It's going to be a lot, so make sure they're there, nephew."

"Alright 'preciate it Uncle D."

"Did you get the reports of the money that was in the bank?"

"Yes sir, I did. So what we looking like as of now Unc?"

"Well after the purchase of the plane, you and your brother's account right now is a little over five hundred million."

Even though they were on the phone and couldn't see each other, a smile formed on both of their faces.

"Alright, unc. I'll talk to you later and my men will be there at noon."

"Alright, nephew, stay up, G," Duran said.

"You too," Kevion said before they both hung up.

"Damn! We done came a long way," Kevion said while looking in his rearview mirror talking to himself.

He called his brother and gave him a recap of his conversation with Duran, then added, "Alright, ain't no time to slack up now; if anything, we gotta tighten up. Have everybody at the airstrip at twelve tomorrow; we got another shipment in."

When the plane arrived the next day, everyone was shocked at how big it was.

"Damn! G, that's one of them muthafuckas that be transporting cars and shit," TK said.

"Yea, that's a big son of a bitch," JoJo commented.

"Where's Kevion or Devion?" Cleopatra asked as she arrived with two moving trucks. She'd driven one and Zolandria was driving the other.

"They 'pose to meet us at the warehouse," TK said.

"Yea, Mickey was meeting them there at eleven, so they wanted to take care of that before we got there," JoJo said.

"Alright, well let's get this bad boy unloaded," Cleopatra said.

With the whole crew there except for the Love Boys, they didn't finish unloading the plane and loading all the product into the truck until 2:30.

When they finished, TK said, "Hey JoJo, call up KD and tell them we on our way and should be there in thirty."

"Yo they on they way back there now," JoJo said.

When they arrived at the warehouse, Kevion opened the doors to the trucks. He looked at all the dope inside, then glanced at the space in their warehouse.

*Damn! Is all this going to fit?* Kevion thought.

"Don't worry, it'll fit," Cleopatra said reading his thoughts.

He laughed. " Damn! What are you? A mind reader now!" Before she could answer, he added, "Oh I get it, you related to Miss Cleo, huh?" Kevion said still laughing.

"I just read people," Cleopatra said. "By the look on your face, you looked like you weren't sure if there would be enough room."

"Yea, it looks like it's gon' be a little tight," Devion said.

"No, Papi, the ceiling is higher than the truck so we will be okay."

"A'ight, let's get to work," Devion said to the crew. "As fast as we get it in, the faster we get it out, and the faster we get this money, baby."

"Right on," Noah said.

"Let's get dis cheddar," Nick agreed.

# Chapter 23

"Damn G! It's been almost a whole year now since we been fuckin' with Duran, bro." Devion said.

"Look where we at, bro. We got mo' money than a lil bit. We got houses in the Caribbean Islands, you got a lil one 'bout to be born and shit. Man, we are on the top of the world," Devion continued while talking to his brother in the office at the club.

Kevion sipped on a drink and smoked a blunt. "We did it, bro, I can't wait till Pops get out to ball with us, though."

"Yea me too, bro, but dig, he ain't got that much to do. He'll be home before we can blink an eye. In the meantime in between time, we gotta stay on point so we can be here when he touch down."

Kevion nodded.

"So far, them faggot ass pigs been straight on they word though. So as long as they happy, we'll be straight, ya feel me?"

Kevion nodded again and said. "That's what's up, but hey, let's go enjoy the night with the rest of the crew celebrating this upcoming anniversary."

Since Hershey was showing with her pregnancy, she sat in the VIP lounge with Kevion, Devion, Honey and the rest of the crew. Kevion had insisted on a DNA test before the baby was even born, and so he had peace of mind knowing that in fact, she was carrying his son. While the rest of the crew popped bottles, smoked and got dances from the finest girls working in the club, the Love Boys sat back and enjoyed themselves seeing others happy, having fun, and on top of their game.

Local rap artists Gator Man, Z-Ro, Sugar-Free, and their entourage were also in attendance chillin' in their VIP booths coming to greet the Love Boys and chop it up with them. Everyone was impressed with the twins and what they'd accomplished.

Since Hershey was getting tired, she told Kevion that she wanted to go home and he gave her the keys to his apartment, walked her out to the front of the club as the valet brought her car around. He kissed her on the forehead and said,

"Be safe on your way to the crib. I know you may be tempted to stop and get your fat ass some snacks, but don't do it. It's too late for you to be getting out your car alone. You hear me, little girl?"

"Yes Daddy, I hear you. I'll be careful." She replied with a smirk on her face.

Since she was so exhausted, she was glad to be going home. She'd be able to rest before Kevion came home – she knew he still had a long night at the club and would come home horny as usual. She came to a red light and leaned back against the headrest waiting for the light to change. She was too tired to pay attention to her surroundings; that's why she didn't notice the two vans that pulled up, one on each side of her.

The sliding door of the van on her driver's side slid open and a man in a ski mask jumped out carrying a large gun.

It didn't even take him a second to shoot a single bullet into her window, shattering the glass, though he missed hitting her on purpose.

At first, she was too shocked to scream, but by the time Hershey realized what was going on, the man pulled open her door and dragged her from the car. Before she could even resist, he slammed the butt of his gun into her temple, causing her to lose consciousness.

Someone from the other van jumped out and into her car. By the time he took off, Hershey was already in the other van, still unconscious as they took her away.

After about forty-five minutes, one of the guys took Hershey's phone and texted Kevion.

*Baby, I made it, see you later.*

When Kevion received the text message, he turned his attention back to his brother and crew who were still hanging at the club with him.

When the club closed, he went to IHOP with the rest of the crew. They stayed out so late that since they had a meeting with Duran at ten, everybody just went from IHOP to the safe house to continue the celebration.

They went from partying to work, first meeting with Duran, then meeting with Juan to deliver another massive shipment. Finally, the brothers sent the crew home to rest.

"Damn bro, all that partying got a nigga tired as hell," Kevion said.

"Yea, I feel you, bro," Devion said. "I'm 'bout to go to the pad, kid.

"I don't think I even have enough energy to even jump in some of that pregnant pussy," Kevion said laughing.

"Yea, laugh that shit off, nigga cuz I know you lying. Better enjoy it while it last cuz lil shawty 'bout to make his entrance in a few, bro," Devion said.

"Alright family, I'm a get at you later, bro," Kevion said. "Hit me up," he said before he hopped into his car.

By the time, he got to his apartment complex's parking lot, Kevion noticed that Hershey's car wasn't in her usual spot.

"Fuck," he said. "Where this girl at?" Then, he thought about it for a moment. *She probably got a craving with her fat ass and went to get something to eat.*

Making it into his door, Kevion decided to take a shower so that he would be fresh when she got back. He walked into his bedroom and noticed that the bed was still made the same as he made it the day before. He studied the room some more: No clothes on the floor or in the bathroom.

Grabbing his phone, he texted her, *Baby girl where you at, ma? If you out getting something to eat, grab me something too, shawty."*

Then, he headed into the kitchen and grabbed a Corona out of the fridge.

After he had popped the top with his bottle opener, a text came back. He smiled, thinking that it was Hershey. While taking a swig from the beer, he read it. He read it the first time, then dropped his bottle, causing the beer to shatter on the kitchen floor.

He read the text again: *Surprise! Surprise! Bitch ass nigga! I got your bitch and unborn seed! How much are they worth to you? If you ever wanna see them again, best do what I say or else…my nigga. Keep the phone on you and don't bother calling. I'll be in touch.*

Kevion read the text again, trying to make sense of it and shouted, "Man! What the fuck!"

Right away, he called Devion.

"Damn, bro," Devion said answering the phone. "I told you to hit me up, but I meant after I woke up, what's tha biz, bro?"

"Man, she ain't here, bro!" Kevion shouted. "My shawty ain't here! Man, somebody got her, bro!"

"Man, she probably at the store, bro calm down," Devion said.

"Naw bro, I just got a text from whoever got her, bro, she ain't here, bro."

# Chapter 24

Kevion seemed to almost pace a hole through his brother's illustrious large living room floor. Three days had passed and not one time had Kevion gotten the telephone call that he'd been so desperately waiting on for the last 72 hours. It had been 68 hours to be exact.

Devion was laying on the couch between Honey's legs with his shirt off and a bottle of Bacardi in his left hand. It pained him to see his brother in so much agony, but he knew there was nothing neither he nor his brother could do at this moment. Nothing but wait to hear from the kidnappers and find out what their demands were.

"Say Bro! Calm down my nig. We gone get your shorty's back" Devion said while extending the blunt he held in this right hand to Kevion. "Here take a smoke."

Kevion put his hand up indicating he did not want the blunt and said "Calm down? Nigga how in the fuck am I supposed to do that when Hershey and my unborn child are somewhere being held against their will? Bro look, the only thing that's on my mind is murdering whoever the fuck got's mine. Either way, it go, whether I get'em back or not, I ain't resting until everyone involved Pay's tha piper." Kevion turned and stared out of a window gripping two glock forties while a vein bulged in his neck.

"I know where you at wit this bro, but look, I'ma need you to remain focused. Nigga soon as we get the green light and we find out who it is it's gonna be straight smash mode" Devion said while exhaling the potent weed smoke from his nostrils.

Devion sat up to put the ashes from his cigar in the ashtray when Kevion's phone began to ring on the coffee table. Kevion walked quickly towards the phone putting the Glock in his right hand in the waistband of his chocolate brown linen pants.

"Who is it?" Kevion asked since Devion had already picked up the phone to look at the caller ID screen.

"I don't know. It's showing up as Unavailable" Devion said while stretching out his arm towards Kevion to give him the phone.

The phone was on the third ring when Kevion swiped the touchscreen to accept the call. Kevion put the phone up to his ear and listened quietly instead of saying Hello. He decided to listen for any background noise or clues that could possibly divulge where the call was coming from before they realized he was on the phone.

A few tense seconds went by and neither the caller nor Kevion said a word.

Devion looked at his brother just holding the phone and mouthed "Who is it?"

At that moment, the silence broke.

"Oh I tink he wants to be a rude boy" A voice said with a deep Jamaican accent. "I don't tink tha boy loves you gurl." The man continued.

As the caller spoke, Kevion's eyes searched frantically to figure out if this was a voice he was familiar with. But he could not place the voice or tie it to any of his previous dealings.

Kevion finally spoke. "Look, let's cut all tha bullshit and get down to business. We can do this the easy way or you can make it difficult on yourself and deal with me the hard way." Kevion said sternly. "You have something I want, so tell me exactly what it is that you want from me so we can all move on past the situation at hand. " Kevion narrowed his eyes and continued. "I must warn you, though, when I find her, and trust me I will, if so much as a hair is disturbed or missing from her head, you will pay dearly."

Devion and Honey were looking at him with a look of astonishment on their faces. In a low voice Devion said, "Bro I don't know if it's a good idea for you to be threatening whoever has your girl, but okay, I'm rolling wit cha."

"Oh is dat rite? Is dat a fact or a promise?" The Jamaican man asked sarcastically.

Before Kevion could respond to the question, he heard Hershey scream in the background.

Devion knew his brother had made a mistake when he saw Kevion's eyes close and the muscles in his jaw started to contract.

Gripping the gun in his left-hand tighter and lightly tapping the trigger, Kevion regained his composure and decided to play along in the sick game the abductor chose to play.

"What is it you want?" Kevion asked.

"You're such a rude boy. See wat you made me do? I don't want to hurt dis beautiful black queen, but yo mouth and threats, I don't take lightly Bumbaclot. Now dat I have your attention, let's talk about what you already took from me and how we can call it even."

"I ain't took nothing from you, nigga! Hell, I don't even know you!" Kevion said loudly.

"Oh Yes, Mon! Yes, you did take someting from me. Dat was my son who took that hit and was supposed to kill you and your brother. Now do you rememba?"

"You are right mon. You don't know me," the caller said. "Allow me to introduce myself. My name is Ba'ki Raaka. I am the father of the man who was paid to assassinate you and your brother. My son, Marley Raaka, who you killed."

Kevion's eyes widened before he said "So how you gone be mad at us for protecting our lives? Me and my brother, to my knowledge, have never intentionally brought any harm to you or your family. Hell, your punk ass son stepped to us!" Kevion yelled into the phone.

Devion looked puzzled at his brother and said, "Who the hell is that who got Hershey?"

Kevion raised his hand in the air to cut Devion off.

Kevion took a deep breath and tried to calm himself before speaking his next words. "Look, I am sorry that you had to lose your son due to the fact that he gambled with his life, but I cannot apologize for the fact that he and not me or my brother are dead. If the shoe was on the other foot and I was feeling the pain that you are experiencing, I don't feel there would be anything that could replace or accommodate for the loss of a loved one. Especially not retaliation against someone who was totally innocent in the situation. We both know your son took a gamble and he lost. He was well aware of the possible outcomes when he chose to become an assassin."

"Shut the fuck up with all that bitch ass bullshit. You and I both know how the street game is played. The taker eventually gets taken." Ba'ki replied. "If you plan on this woman and your child staying alive, you will not get the police involved and you will do exactly as I say."

"So what is it that you want?" Kevion said walking towards the window.

"Listen, I am a businessman, so I have a proposition for you that will ensure your ladies safety. That is if you accept the terms of what I have to offer, of course."

"A proposition? What fucking type of proposition could you possibly have in mind for me?"

There was a brief moment of silence before the Jamaican continued.

"It's simple. I'm willing to trade her life, for yours." Ba'ki said. "I targeted you, instead of your brother, because you are the mastermind behind The Love Boys operation. Without you, your brother will be dead from his own undoing in a matter of months."

Kevion clenched his jaws, glanced over at his brother and then turned back to look out the window. "I'm listening muthafucka."

"If this lady isn't of any value to you, I'll settle for her life and then you will be able to pick her up piece by piece from off one of the highways after I carve her up like a holiday turkey."

A few seconds went by as Kevion hung his head, contemplating the sacrifice he had to make for Hershey and his unborn child.

"So what is it going to be Bumbaclot?" Ba'ki asked breaking Kevion's train of thought.

"Just tell me when and where?" Kevion replied staring out of the window.

"Damn gul! He really does love you." Ba'ki said talking to Hershey. "Kevion I'll tell you what. I'm going to allow you 24 hours to say your goodbye's and spend some time with your family, starting now. It's 7 o'clock and at 6:30 tomorrow I will text you the location for you to meet me. And rude boy, make sure you come alone!" Ba'ki shouted as he hung up the phone.

Kevion looked at the blank screen on his cell phone as rage and tears fought for supreme position in his eyes. He walked past Devion and Honey without saying a word.

"So what's the deal bro?" Devion asked rising from the couch, following his brother into the kitchen, with Honey following behind.

"God Damn KD bro! Tell me something. Is Hershey still alive or what?" Devion asked with a sense of urgency in his voice.

"Yeah, she's still alive bro," Kevion replied while placing his pistol on the granite countertop of the large island in the kitchen, before grabbing a bottle of water from the refrigerator.

"So what's up bro? What that mufucka talking about?" Devion said, obviously annoyed by his brother's lack of communication.

Kevion walked quietly over to the bar and sat on a stool. Adding to the thick layer of suspense in the air.

"So what's going on brother-in-law? Is my girl gonna be okay?" Honey asked with concern.

Kevion massaged his temple and said, "Yeah Honey, she's gone be straight. I'm going to get her back tomorrow."

"Tomorrow! Why the fuck we ain't getting her today?" Devion asked.

"Look, after he told me he was going to text me where to meet him tomorrow, the mufucka hung up the phone on me before I could ask the same question myself." Kevion lied. "But look, this is what I need you to do. Call everybody and have them meet us at the safe house. Have T.K. get in touch with his boy Markel. I think I can use his expertise on this one". Kevion said as he took out his phone and dialed a telephone number.

# Chapter 25

**K**evion pulled up to the location Ba'ki had texted him earlier. It was an abandoned warehouse near White Rock Lake. Dusk was starting to set in which made the secluded area seem like a picturesque ghost town. He had purposely arrived 15 minutes earlier than the agreed time in hopes of gaining some leverage in the doomsday situation. He was alone, but his brother and crew were actually on the other side of the lake watching the dangerous exchange.

Kevion stepped out of his black Porsche truck and surveyed his surroundings. "Nothing so far," he said into his telephone Bluetooth earpiece with Devion on the other end.

"Okay. We got eyes on you bro and our Thirty-Thirty's with scopes are pointed that way. If anything pop-off we are ready to knock they socks off." Devion replied.

Kevion opened the back door of his truck and pulled out a large black duffle bag. He placed it on the hood of the truck and unzipped it carefully to check the contents. Before he zipped it up, he retrieved an iPad from the console of his car and placed it next to the bag. He wasn't sure if he was more pissed or afraid of this impending confrontation. About that time a white Five Hundred Mercedes-Benz began driving towards the warehouse where Kevion was parked.

"You see em'? " Kevion said into the earpiece.

"Yeah we got eyes on that muthfuca," Devion said. "Handle yo business."

Hershey was in the back seat but spotted Kevion as the Benz drove on the gravel roadway. Knowing her man and his trigger-happy brother, she did not know what to expect during this confrontation. She was just so happy to see her man again. She had cried relentlessly when she woke up in unknown surroundings after being knocked unconscious during the kidnapping, but her abductor had assured her that it was not his intention to hurt her. She only began to question his motives after he pulled her hair and jerked her neck when speaking with Kevion on the phone. That had left her cautious and afraid of his capabilities.

As they drove down the road toward the warehouse, Hershey looked over at her abductor with mixed feelings. On one hand she felt some pity for him because he was obviously taking the loss of his son really hard. He had been consumed with anguish and pain the entire time she was in his custody. On the other hand, she was angry with him for choosing to take her as a hostage and risking the life of her unborn child. Every time she thought about how close that bullet came to killing her while at the red light that night, she felt nauseous.

"So what's about to happen now?" Hershey asked.

"You ask a lot of questions for someone in your position," Ba'ki replied. "If your punk ass boyfriend is a man of his word, I'll be back in Jamaica with a lighter burden in no time."

Hershey had been trying to figure out the plan ever since she was pulled out of the room in the middle of Ba'kis conversation with Kevion. She could not hear them very well, but she could have sworn she heard something about a trade.

"Stop right here" Ba'ki instructed the driver. "Get out and go check him to make sure he is not packing heat."

The driver stopped the car with the headlights shining directly on Kevion. He and the other bodyguard in the passenger seat got out and approached him.

Kevion held up his hands, in anticipation of what was about to happen. He had a feeling that the Jamaican would want to be sure he was not walking into an ambush, so he left his gun on the front seat of his truck. His main concern was getting Hershey and his unborn child back safely.

"I'm clean muthafucka and I am alone just like you instructed. Now let my girl go and cut out all the bullshit." Kevion said sounding vexed.

The bodyguard from the passenger seat walked back to the Mercedes and opened the right rear door. The Jamaican emerged from the car unaccompanied.

Devion was looking in the high-powered binoculars and saw the distinct resemblance of the man who got out the backseat with the man who tried to kill him in the Waffle House parking lot.

"Oh, it's ShowTime muthafuckas. That's his bitch ass father for sure. He got the same long fat nose and just as blue- black as his dead ass son." Devion said enraged. "If this muthafucka even blink wrong, we gonna light his ass up."

Kevion remained in his spot with the driver's mini AK-47 pointed at him.

The man walked toward Kevion, leaving the bodyguard behind at the car.

Feeling the tension in the air, the man motioned for the driver to lower his gun and he extended his hand toward Kevion.

A few seconds passed with Kevion fighting back the urge to grab the man by the throat and snatch his life right out of him.

"Do you really think I'm about to shake hands with a muthafucka who has forced me into a suicidal situation? You must be out of your Rastafarian mind". Kevion spat. "My father taught me to shake hands with a man I respect. I ain't got no form of respect for a man who terrorizes pregnant women. Speaking of which, where is my girl? I held up my end of the bargain. Where is she?"

Ba'ki raised his right hand with his finger in the air and moved it in a circular motion. The bodyguard acknowledged his signal, opened the rear door and Hershey emerged, slapping away the helping hand of the oversized guard. She quickly scanned the area until her eyes locked onto Kevion's. She walked as quickly as her 8-month pregnant body would allow. Her ankles were swollen and she was exhausted from the entire ordeal.

Kevion's jaw stiffened and contracted with each step she took. It took everything within him not to run towards Hershey and carry her in his arms.

"I'll allow you a moment to say your goodbyes," Ba'ki said as he saw the pain written on Kevion's face.

"I just need to get her into my truck and let her leave before you do whatever it is you have planned for me. That's all I ask." Kevion said clinching his jaw.

Hershey finally reached Kevion after walking twenty steps which to her felt like twenty miles. Kevion met her the last five steps and grabbed her, holding her very tightly.

"Are you okay baby?" Kevion asked with tears in his eyes.

"Yeah, baby. I'm straight. Just ready to go home." Hershey replied.

"Okay love. Let me get you in the truck." Kevion said while placing a kiss on her forehead.

When Kevion and Hershey reached his truck, to Hershey's surprise, he opened his driver door to let her inside.

"Okay love. Go ahead, get in and don't ask any questions." Kevion said sternly.

"But, what is..." Hershey began to ask.

Kevion cut her off before she could finish her question. "No questions. When I tell you to drive off, just do it. If needed, Devion will explain everything to you later."

Tears began to stream down Hershey's face as she looked at Kevion trying to understand what was going on.

Kevion closed the truck door and walked back over towards Ba'ki.

"I thank you for releasing her according to our agreement, but I want you to know I am a man of my word also," Kevion said with contention in his voice.

Looking confused, Ba'ki said, "And what do you mean by that?"

"You see Ba'ki, I think it's time that we renegotiate our deal," Kevion replied with a slight smirk on his face.

"And why would I do that?" Ba'ki asked with aggravation.

"How about this, why don't you have one of your Terry Crews looking muthafuckas go over to my truck and get that iPad I have sitting on the hood. I think it will be better for me to show you. That way you'll be able to grasp the magnitude of the situation and then you can decide where we go from there."

Ba'kis eyes narrowed as he looked at Kevion and signaled for his driver to go and retrieve the device.

"And while you at it, go ahead and bring that duffle bag back with you," Kevion yelled over his shoulder.

As the driver walked back carrying the bag and iPad, Ba'ki couldn't help but notice the concerned look plastered on his guards face.

The guard dropped the bag between Kevion and Ba'ki, then handed his boss the electronic device.

"So what's it going to be Ba'ki? How do you want to do this?" Kevion asked as he noticed Ba'ki's face do the impossible by turning a few shades lighter as he looked down at the image on the iPad screen in his hands. "Because I promise," Kevion continued, "If my crew hears the tiniest bit of distress coming from me, at the other end of this Bluetooth device in my ear, you can best believe it's going to be curtains for them."

Ba'ki was speechless as his eyes swelled with tears. Within seconds, the tears began to splatter on top of the image of his wife and two daughters, naked, on their knees with tape covering their mouths and their hands tied in front of them. There were six Hispanic looking men standing behind them with five guns drawn to their heads while the sixth rested a machete on his shoulder.

"Bitch ass nigga! Stop crying and look at me." Kevion shouted while snatching the iPad from Ba'ki's tight grip. "I'm willing to let you and your family live. That is if that's what you want. See right now, you still have the upper hand on my life. You could make the bold decision to still kill me and sacrifice your family. But do me a favor and look down at your heart right now."

When Devion heard his brother's cue, he and the crew with him turned the beams of their guns toward Ba'ki and his bodyguards. Placing a red dot right in the center of their chests.

"But if I die, Well, I think you get the picture," Kevion explained.

Ba'ki narrowed his eyes, walked closer to Kevion and said, "Bumbaclot, you really don't know who you are fucking wit."

"No, you don't know who you are fucking with, old man. I suggest you take this 20 mill I have in this duffle bag and get the fuck out of here. Go back to your family and enjoy the mercy I'm willing to extend to you. For what it's worth, I do apologize for your son's death, but you must admit he made his bed. I can only hope he made that muthafucka comfortable before he decided to fuck with me and mine."

Without another word, Ba'ki signaled for his driver to retrieve the bag.

"You have my word that by the time you get home, your family will be waiting on you." Kevion continued.

Ba'ki returned to his car as one of his henchmen held the door open for him. Kevion watched as all three men got into the car, turned around on the gravel roadway and drove off.

"You see that shit bro?" Kevion said into his earpiece.

"Yeah, bro I saw and heard the whole thing," Devion replied. "It took everything within me not to peel his wig back. Damn!"

The Mercedes had driven about half a mile from the meeting location when **BOOM!** An explosion rocked the car and shook the ground where Kevion was still standing. He had activated the remote for the bomb that was in the duffle bag he gave to Ba'ki. His boy Markel was ex-military and came out with the nickname "Boom" for his bomb-making skills. The Love Boys had learned in their business, a variety of firepower tended to be a necessity from time to time.

"Yo D-Mac," Kevion said into his earpiece.

"Yeah, what's up bro?"

"Tell Juan I said closed casket," Kevion said referring to Ba'ki's wife and daughters.

"I told you his bitch ass was going to pay! Don't nobody fuck with The Love Boys and think they just get to walk away. He got us all the way fucked up!" Kevion spat as he walked back to his truck.

□

# Chapter 26

**A** month had passed since the kidnapping incident. Hershey had taken a while to feel completely safe and resume' the ability to sleep soundly without having nightmares. The birth of their son, Ma'Kai, had aided in the recovery process as well.

Kevion had left much of the business to Devion, since getting Hershey back safely. He was just a little too paranoid to leave her and Ma'Kai alone so soon after the abduction. Devion had gotten all of their business back on track. He took care of the Cartel by providing them with some extra product for their assistance with Ba'ki's family in Jamaica. He also checked in with Duran and got their next shipment scheduled so they could make sure they had the funds to make their monthly payment to Detective's Dotson and Johnson. Besides they owed them a little extra since they had managed for the DNA found in Ba'ki's car, which tied back to them, to mysteriously disappear. Luckily they had been the detectives assigned to the case and had since ruled the explosion an accident due to mechanical failure of the car's gas line.

Devion was home watching television when a story flashed across the screen that caught his attention. He immediately picked up the phone and called Kevion, who was at their vacation home in The Cayman Islands with Ma'Kai, Hershey, their mom, grandmother, and great-grandmother.

"Say bro turn the TV on CNN and check the news out," Devion said.

"Aight, hold up," Kevion said, shifting Ma'Kai to his other arm while he reached for the remote control.

The news story read: *The State of Louisiana is shortening the time and releasing inmates that are being held on non-violent charges due to overcrowding and unfair sentencing practices. The first round of inmates are being released as early as this week.*

"You see that shit bro?" Devion said excitedly as he smoked on his blunt.

"Yea I see it, but I wonder if that has anything to do with Dad," Kevion said.

"I'm not sure, but it should" Devion replied. "I'll admit that they got him on some stupid bullshit that he did, but it did not involve guns or anything violent. No way he should have gotten the time the judge handed down to him."

"Yea, you right about that bro. I think that was the work of g-gram's prayers. You know he's always told us how she prays that he gets caught if he does anything wrong." Kevion said shaking his head.

"Yeah, I remember bro. I just be hoping she ain't praying the same thing about us." Devion said while blowing the weed smoke from his nostrils. "Hopefully since we the great-grands she lets us slide with them Christian special requests she be sending up."

"For sho,'" Kevion said laughing loudly and slightly startling Ma'Kai.

"Just in case, I'm about to call his lawyer and see what's up," Devion said.

"Cool. I'll check with moms and see if she heard anything about it. We both know she and dad are good at keeping stuff from us. For all we know, he could already have a revised release date. Knowing how smart and slick our old man is, he may have gotten with the politicians and made this new law happen."

"You know your ass is right about that," Devion said smiling. "Aight, I'll hit you back later. One."

"Yeah, it was something else I meant to tell you, but this news on CNN made me forget. I'll think of it and call you back. One". Kevion said before hanging up the phone.

*Damn Pops. I hope you finna come home, nigga. We got shit to do out'chere. I know once you touch down, everything gonna be straight.* Devion said to himself as he picked up the phone to dial the number to his father's attorney. Before he could dial the number, his phone rang. Without looking at the Caller ID he answered.

"What up bro? You remember what you had to tell me?"

"Sorry to disappoint you, but this ain't your brother." The caller said with a Jamaican accent.

"Who is this?" Devion said as he looked at the screen on his phone which showed *Unavailable*.

"Trust me. You will find out soon enough. I only called to inform you that you missed one." The caller replied.

*******************************

As the private jet came to its resting state on the runway after a smooth landing, the pilot spoke. "Sir, we have arrived at your destination. The car service previously arranged is waiting for you ahead."

"Thank You, Jonathan."

"It's good to have you back, sir. I'm sure your family will be ecstatic about your return as well. Enjoy your stay in The Cayman Islands, Mr. Robinson."

Made in the USA
San Bernardino, CA
24 September 2018